The
Unexpected
Resolution

Elaine L. Orr

THE UNEXPECTED RESOLUTION
ELAINE L. ORR

BOOK 10 OF THE
JOLIE GENTIL COZY MYSTERY SERIES

The Unexpected Resolution is a work of fiction. All characters and events are products of the author's imagination.

www.elaineorr.com
www.elaineorr.blogspot.com

Library of Congress Control Number: 2017909720
ISSBN 978-0-9863380-6-9

ACKNOWLEDGMENTS

Thanks to the Decatur critique group – Angela, Dave, Debbie, Marilyn, and both Sues. I am truly grateful for first readers, especially my sister, Diane Orr-Fisher, and author Karen Musser Nortman. Finally, I appreciate the good humor of the staff in the three places I'm most likely to write – in Chatham, Illinois, the Public Library and Edgar's Coffee Shop; in Springfield, the Starbucks on Freedom Drive.

DEDICATION

To family members and friends who have encouraged my writing, with special thanks to the late Lynn Larkin. She passed her love of books to countless readers.

CHAPTER ONE

YOU CAN FREEZE YOUR BUNS OFF in December at the Jersey Shore. That's why all the tourism brochures feature seagulls on the beach in July.

I shouldn't have been surprised that December thirtieth was a good day to freeze my toes, or feet, or any other part of my anatomy. But that didn't mean I liked it. Especially the whisper of snow that had begun to hit my windshield. I wanted to finish grocery shopping and take the food to Aunt Madge's Cozy Corner B&B before the snow storm blew in later.

On Christmas day, Scoobie and I told Aunt Madge and her husband, Harry, that we were not only getting married, but we were going to be parents next year.

Scoobie and I are so excited it's hard to keep silly smiles off our faces. Okay, his is full-time smiling. I'm a little afraid I won't be a good mom. I haven't said that out loud though. When I stop throwing up every morning I'll probably be more confident.

As I got out of the car in the lot beside Mr. Markle's In-Town Grocery, I sniffed. The breeze came from the ocean, crisp freshness with every breath.

My grocery list included a mix of frozen hors d'oeurves, oranges, cake mixes, confectioners' sugar, ginger ale, refrigerator rolls, and Vienna sausages. All the ingredients for an informal wedding reception – if your fiancé wants the food to include pigs-in-a-blanket.

I had almost reached the sidewalk in front of the store when a loud voice boomed across the parking lot. Waving at me was Max, who wore a red stocking cap that sported reindeer antlers. "Jolie, Jolie. You and Scoobie are getting married. Married."

Max received a traumatic brain injury during the Iraq War. As TBIs go, his could be a lot worse, I suppose. He can live on his own, with support from friends, but his overall attitude is childlike. And he repeats himself. A lot.

I pulled my scarf tighter as I gestured for Max to come into the store with me. I hurried in and made for the coffee pot Mr. Markle keeps ready for customers. *Rats. No decaf.*

Max swung the door open with his characteristic enthusiasm and grinned broadly. He is about five-six and not particularly good-looking. Because he is almost always cheerful, that's what most people notice.

It's good to keep Max busy, so I grabbed a shopping cart and shoved it in his direction. "I'm so glad to see you. You want to push my cart?"

"I do, I do. Do you have a list?"

I almost laughed. Scoobie has been teaching Max how to shop on a budget, and list-making took a while for Max to grasp. I pulled a folded paper from my pocket and he grabbed it as he began to push the cart.

"I know where everything is now." He stopped to study the list. "What are refrigerator rolls?"

"You keep them in the fridge until you're ready to cook them. They come in a round can."

Max studied me. "All cans are round. Round."

I grinned. "True. I meant as opposed to the kind of rolls that are kept on the shelves, by the loaves of bread."

He absorbed that and started for the produce aisle. Max loves fruit. I saw bananas and grapes in my future, in addition to the oranges.

I unbuttoned my parka and waved at Mr. Markle, several aisles away. The green linoleum floors are old and the aisles narrow, but he keeps the place impeccably clean and will order anything he doesn't regularly stock.

"Thank you for inviting me to your wedding. To your wedding. Scoobie said you are squeezing people to fit in Aunt Madge's house. Her house."

"Her great room, to be exact. You've been in it, the huge space that has her living room, dining room, and kitchen all together."

"And the door to let the dogs out. Into the back yard. The back yard."

We moved from produce to baking supplies, one of Max's favorite aisles.

"You have parents, Jolie, parents."

Scoobie must have told him they were not coming up from Florida. "Yes, but my father broke his ankle two weeks ago. My mom doesn't want to come without

3

him." *Thank God.* "But they'll listen on the phone. They'll sort of be there."

"I know your sister."

I noted the lack of repetition. Unusual. "Yes. I think you met Renée and her daughters and maybe her husband one year on Halloween. They live in Lakewood, where I used to live."

"But Aunt Madge is your maid of honor. Of honor."

"Yes, well, Renée is my sister and my best friend, but Aunt Madge and I have gotten really close since I moved back to Ocean Alley. If I hadn't lived with her for a while, I never would have reconnected with Scoobie."

"Aunt Madge married Harry. Harry."

"She did." I've worked for Harry for several years, as a real estate appraiser. We've managed the transition to more than boss and employee well. I occasionally am more persistent about things than Harry would like. I'm working on that.

Max and I finished filling the cart, which now included a box of Cocoa Puffs. Scoobie got him hooked on those.

Mr. Markle seemed to be the only one working at the moment, because he joined us at the cash register. "You're looking good Jolie."

I blushed. "You heard the news?"

He smiled fully, rare for him. "Your aunt's reputation as closed-mouthed is out the window."

"Where did it go? Go?" Max asked.

"Remember Scoobie talked to you about 'expressions' that are not literal? Mr. Markle means

Aunt Madge's reputation for not being much of a big talker has changed."

Before Max could answer, I looked at Mr. Markle. "In fact I'm buying some of the food to eat after the ceremony."

He looked up the price of oranges before ringing up the six I had. "Getting married at First Prez?"

"Too much like work."

He nodded. "You and that First Prez Food Pantry."

"It's called Harvest for All," Max said. "For everybody. Jolie makes it work. Jolie works."

Max can sometimes try people's patience. Mr. Markle's frown said this was one of those times.

"We're getting married at Aunt Madge's. Not a big group." Every time I said this I wondered if people were offended not to be invited. Scoobie always tells me that I create my own guilt.

He started to bag the groceries. "Is Reverend Jamieson officiating?"

"We asked him, but he always goes to his sister's in Massachusetts the week after Christmas. You know, it doesn't take long to get certified to officiate a wedding." I looked away from Mr. Markle's gaze.

He paused, seemingly thinking. "Harry?"

I swallowed. "George."

Never had I heard Mr. Markle laugh. He leaned his head back and put a hand on the apron covering his ample stomach.

Max looked at me. "Is George funny? Funny?"

I murmured, "He thinks so."

George Winters is Scoobie's best friend. He used to be a reporter for the *Ocean Alley Press*, and would bug the daylights out of me if I looked into how a local person turned into a corpse. Probably Mr. Markle's laugh was because George and I also dated briefly.

Mr. Markle wiped a tear with the back of his hand. "Got certified pretty fast, did he?"

"I, uh, think Scoobie let him in on the deal before he told me. Or asked me."

CHAPTER TWO

AS I STOOD IN AUNT MADGE'S spacious kitchen reading the directions on a cake mix box, I smiled to myself. In Scoobie's typical lack of concern about tradition, guests would eat before the ceremony. We would exchange vows at exactly midnight, thus welcoming in the New Year.

Actually, my father suggested January might be a better month to get married than December. Something about financial planning and taxes. We didn't care, but my father felt pretty helpless down in Florida, so we accepted his advice.

Scoobie thought of the New Year's Eve party that would culminate in our nuptials. Though, as he put it, I couldn't have champagne at either event.

He was having a blast with wedding preparation, even though we had a compressed timeframe. I hadn't abdicated the planning. I felt bone-tired a lot, and my husband-to-be was brimming with ideas.

Aunt Madge came through the swinging door from the breakfast room into her kitchen. "Are you making the cakes today?"

"I thought I might. They should still be fresh tomorrow." Scoobie and I had decided to have several kinds, but made in rectangular pans, nothing fancy. We were saving money in the hope of moving from our tiny bungalow into something bigger before the baby entered our lives.

Aunt Madge turned on her electric kettle and pulled a tea bag from a canister on the counter. "I wish you would let me do scratch cakes."

I lifted an orange as if about to throw it at her. "You are a guest, not the caterer. The matron of honor will have many duties." I nodded at her foot, in its walking cast. "Plus, she limps."

Except for falling off a kitchen stool while hanging garland a few weeks ago, which netted her a hairline wrist fracture and broken ankle, Aunt Madge is as steady as a rock. My rock.

She did a more or less ladylike snort. Aunt Madge is in her mid-eighties, and technically is my great aunt. She looks about seventy. Probably the result of decades of being an active B&B owner and volunteering for everything from the hospital auxiliary to First Prez Sunday School.

I love that she dyes her white hair a different color every three weeks or so. She doesn't use permanent color, and has been known to vary the shade based on a dress she plans to wear. Today it was a deep red. Thank heavens she hadn't bought a purple dress for the wedding.

She poured herself a cup of tea as I lined up cake mixes on the counter – three chocolate (think Max), carrot, yellow, and red velvet.

"Will you at least let me make some of the frosting?"

I almost said no, but decided her kitchen would be a lot cleaner if she wielded the confectioners' sugar. "Okay, if you let me help."

She raised one eyebrow, something I've never mastered. "Oh, that would make it go a lot faster." She lifted her wrist, which now sported a removable brace rather than a cast. "I can wash both my hands. Totally sanitary."

I poured myself a cup of tea and we moved to her large oak table, accompanied by my tiny black cat, Jazz. "I wasn't worried about that. You can tell me to melt butter or something."

"It's a deal." We sat, and our gazes met. "You're sure about this?"

"I'm glad I'm sitting down. Why wouldn't I be?"

"Personally, I always hoped you and Scoobie would swim against whatever waves you had to face so that you could end up together. I just don't want you to feel as if you have to rush into things."

"I honestly never thought I would be this happy." My first marriage had ended spectacularly when my ex embezzled money from his employer, a bank, to support a gambling habit I didn't know about. He topped that with raiding our joint retirement savings and not expressing a smidgen of regret.

She mimed checking an item off a list. "That's taken care of."

I grinned at her. "Thanks for asking, though."

Jazz meowed loudly, and I peered under the table. She usually sits by my shoes, but she sat a couple feet away. "I know it's confusing. We don't live here anymore. But you'll be home in a couple of days." She meowed again. "And you get to see the dogs." Though she plays haughty, Jazz grew very fond of Aunt Madge's exuberant retrievers when we lived at the B&B. Mister Rogers and Miss Piggy occasionally visit at our bungalow, or Jazz comes to the B&B for a sleepover.

Before Jazz could respond, the side door to Aunt Madge's large Victorian home banged, and we turned in that direction. The door faces the parking lot and is close to her B&B guests' breakfast area, where we would serve food tomorrow.

Scoobie came through the swinging kitchen door, arms laden with an assortment of pine wreathes. "Sergeant Morehouse called to say they had a bunch of these left at the Saint Anthony's tree lot. We thought they would smell great."

He lined up four wreathes next to each other on the oak table, and cocked his head as he studied them. "I guess we can ditch the red bows in favor of something less Christmassy."

Aunt Madge rubbed her nose, probably trying not to smile. "What kind of ribbons are you getting?"

I did smile. Her message was clear. He brought shedding pine needles into her house, but Scoobie would have to deal with them.

He ran a hand through his dark blonde hair, which sported melting snowflakes. "I'll call Ramona. She's doing decorations."

Our friend Ramona had claimed this as her role, but we didn't know her ideas. As with nearly all of the wedding plans, I had a *laissez-faire* attitude. Perhaps my French ancestry helped. My father chose my name, Jolie Gentil, which is pronounced with a soft J and G. It means pretty nice in French but, thankfully, most people don't know that. I would have to live up to it.

I had stayed seated, so Scoobie bent over to kiss me. "I don't have to work tomorrow."

"That's great!" Aunt Madge and I spoke almost in unison. He'd been scheduled to work New Year's Eve day at his job in the Radiology Department of the Ocean Alley Hospital. Since the holiday work schedule had been planned long before our wedding, Scoobie didn't ask for it off.

"Yeah, that new x-ray tech offered to trade. I'll work for her Presidents' Weekend. I barely know her."

Aunt Madge stood to carry her empty tea mug to the sink. "Good people everywhere." She made a shooing gesture. "Go call Ramona."

When I heard him on the house phone in the breakfast room, I pointed at the wreaths and shrugged at Aunt Madge. "What was he thinking?"

"He's being festive."

I returned to the cake mixes. The wreath donor, Sergeant Morehouse, is someone I've butted heads with from time to time. Mostly we're friendly.

Scoobie stuck his head in the kitchen for three seconds. "I invited Morehouse. That's okay, right?"

To the swinging door, I said, "Uh, sure."

Aunt Madge grinned. "Maybe Scoobie expects to find a body among the wedding presents."

CHAPTER THREE

HE DIDN'T SEEM TO expect a body, but my husband-to-be brimmed with excitement. I glanced around Newhart's Diner, the off-the-boardwalk restaurant that is especially homey in the off-season.

Scoobie planned to meet me for supper. A burger and one of Arnie's famous butterscotch milkshakes for him, and chicken salad for me. I was trying to eat healthier, for the next six months at least.

A woman's voice came from behind me. "Jolie! I heard your news."

Elmira Washington probably caught wind of my internal groan. "Thanks. Scoobie and I are excited."

Elmira stood next to my booth. Same short gray hair, with beady eyes surveying the diner for opportunities to gossip. Her gaze came back to me. "So, Scoobie is the father?"

Elmira would aggravate a puppy. It would do no good to count to ten because I'd be no calmer when I hit the top number. I couldn't keep an edge out of my tone. "Elmira, who else have you seen me with the last year or so?"

She focused on me. I took in her cloth coat, which today sported a coffee stain and whatever she had just eaten. Aunt Madge and I had begun to wonder if Elmira's occasional shakes were becoming Parkinson's tremors. *Patience, Jolie.*

"Well now, you have a point. Are you going to get married or see what it's like to be parents before you try that?"

God give me strength. "You must have heard we have a wedding coming up."

Elmira's brows knitted and she tilted her head. "You know, maybe I did hear that."

Scoobie's voice came from behind Elmira. "Hear what?"

Elmira had the decency to look ill at ease, and I didn't want Scoobie to bear her rudeness. "She's congratulating us on the baby and the wedding."

Scoobie grinned as he slid in across from me. He rubbed his hands together and removed a dark green parka that bore flecks of snow. "I'd say in that order, but we are getting married before the little sucker pops out."

"Oh, my." Elmira backed a step away from the table. "I'll leave you two to get some dinner."

I stuck out my tongue at her retreating back.

Scoobie picked up the menu. "She bugging you?"

"Probably not the most she ever has." Elmira had made sure the entire town knew about my divorce when I arrived on Aunt Madge's doorstep. She is the only person in town I truly dislike.

He looked at me over the top of his menu. "Did she ever get approved for assisted living at Silver Times?"

Elmira had gotten in trouble for sneaking in at night to scout the retirement complex for vacant units. "We'll have to ask Aunt Madge. Elmira might still be on the outs with management over there."

Scoobie deadpanned, "No kidding."

I smiled and shook my head. "Hard to believe Aunt Madge was in there only a week ago. What a difference a walking cast makes."

He nodded, somber now. "I'm worried she'll try to do too much for the wedding."

"Harry said he'll get a fly swatter to keep her out of the kitchen if she stands up too long. He also…"

A waving hand near the entrance caught my attention. Max gestured enthusiastically from the diner's doorway.

Scoobie turned his head slightly and indicated that Max should join us.

I kept my voice low. "This is getting to be too much of a…good thing."

Scoobie slid over so Max could slide into the booth bench across from me. "I hear you. I think it's excitement about the wedding."

Max grinned as he sat. "Exciting. Very exciting."

I chided myself for being a grouch. "It is. I'm trying not to be nervous."

"You're never nervous, Jolie. Never nervous."

I smiled. "Mostly I'm not." I glanced behind Max as Elmira moved away from another booth and made for the exit. She waved at the man and young boy she'd been talking to. He was perhaps in his sixties, with thinning brown hair speckled with gray. Between Aunt Madge's friends, my job, and the food pantry, I knew most permanent Ocean Alley residents in that age bracket. Not him.

Scoobie elbowed Max gently. "I thought you liked to be home to watch *Big Bang Theory* at six o'clock."

"I do. *Big Bang*, I do." He almost bounced in his seat. "I saw you go into the diner. The diner."

Scoobie nodded, looking directly at Max. "Are you hungry?"

"Food at home. Home. Megan taught me about the freezer and defrosting." He paused, and frowned. "Frost is outside. Outside."

Megan, who now spends less time as a Harvest for All volunteer because she operates Java Jolt coffee shop, is one of Max's regular advisors. I had to smile. I can't help it when Max is literal. "The freezer is kind of frosty inside. That's why we say defrost when we take out frozen food."

Before Max had a chance to ask another question, Arnie Newhart came to our booth, his order book open. Arnie and his wife have operated Newhart's for decades. They recently gave it a facelift, even putting the myriad of local news stories and photos on neat bulletin boards plastered throughout the diner.

"Blue plate special?"

I shook my head. "I'm eating lighter than meatloaf and mashed potatoes."

Scoobie shut his menu. "Burger, no cheese, well done. And of course," he gestured at me, "a butterscotch milkshake to share with my friend over there."

Arnie shook his head. "Your friend. Congratulations, by the way."

I ordered my chicken salad, Max declined to order, and Arnie headed for the kitchen.

Max slid out of the booth. The diner had grown crowded and he almost ran into a young couple, cheeks red from the cold, who were hurrying to a booth. "So sorry. Sorry."

They barely reacted. I wished they had told Max it was okay, and then reminded myself not to assume other people's feelings. I learned that in a family twelve-step meeting that Scoobie and George dragged me to.

Max put on his bright green mittens. "*Big Bang*. Sheldon."

I grinned at him. "Did you finish learning the song?"

Max frowned. "It's hard. Hard. But I still try."

He walked toward the door, almost bumping into the man Elmira had talked to, who had stood to put on his coat. Max partially blocked the man from my view, but I saw him put an arm on Max's shoulder and seem to say something reassuring to him. *He must be local. He knows Max.*

Scoobie made a whew gesture across his brow. "Love the guy."

"Yep." I pulled out a small notebook. "Last time we have to coordinate."

Scoobie leaned his head back and raised his eyes to the ceiling before looking back at me. "The things I do for my bride."

"Okay, first things first. Who else have you invited?"

GEORGE AND RAMONA JOINED us just as we finished eating. Though George always wears long pants in the winter, as opposed to his usual khaki shorts and Hawaiian shirts, he still manages to look rumpled most of the time.

George took a French fry from Scoobie's plate and motioned that he should move down. "Been looking for you two."

Ramona removed her burgundy cape and smoothed her skirt before sliding in next to me. Only she could get away with the 1960s hippie clothes she wears. As usual, her outfit – tonight a tie-dyed burgundy skirt and tan crocheted vest – went together perfectly.

"What he means," she said, "is he didn't want to be the only one to carry the decorations into the B&B."

"You, uh, have a lot?" I asked.

George grimaced. "My entire back seat."

"Are you hinting Ramona should buy a car?" Scoobie asked.

She refastened her hair in its large clip. "I've never even had a driving lesson."

"I think he just wants to sell you insurance," I said.

George snorted. "I investigate insurance claims, not sell the damn stuff."

Scoobie shoved the plate with its remaining fries to him. "But you won't have to go out New Year's Eve, will you?"

Ocean Alley is small enough that sometimes the local police call George to an accident scene or home burglary. Though they say it's because he'll likely be the insurance investigator called to examine a situation;

mostly it's because he takes better photos than the officers.

"Shouldn't have to. Besides, they all know where I'll be."

I raised my eyebrows at Scoobie. "Is there anyone you haven't told?"

He grinned. "You should get out more. I have to do all the hard work."

"How's the morning sickness?" Ramona asked.

George blanched.

I shrugged. "It's a good thing we're getting married at night."

Scoobie elbowed George. "Did you download the stuff that has to be in the vows?"

"Yep." From his pocket George pulled a paper so wrinkled it looked as if he'd found it in the trash. He noticed my expression. "All I had to write on."

"A guy who writes reports finds himself without paper," I murmured.

"Funny." He shoved the paper toward Scoobie.

I tried not to let my annoyance show. "How come you aren't letting me see?"

George shrugged. "Scoobie promised no funny stuff."

Scoobie looked up from the paper. "So, this is what the state requires. How creative can we be?"

"Probably as much as your bride will let…" George's phone rang and he pulled it from his pocket and stepped away from us.

I raised my eyebrows in Scoobie's direction and turned to Ramona. "You ordering?"

She shook her head. "I have homemade yogurt at home."

Scoobie mimed gagging.

George came back, took one more French fry, but didn't sit. "Gotta go. Accident in front of the Sand Piper."

"My least favorite place," Scoobie said.

I shot him a look of sympathy. His mother spent a lot of time in that bar when Scoobie was young.

Ramona tapped the table with my spoon. "You have the decorations in your car."

George took a drink of Scoobie's water. "See you at the B&B. Won't take long."

Ramona frowned. "Guess I'm with you guys."

Scoobie pulled on his jacket. "We have two cars. You're okay going with the pregnant lady, right?"

Ramona pointed toward the door and I blew him a kiss.

"Why do you suppose he's in such a hurry?" she asked.

"Probably plotting something with George for tomorrow night."

CHAPTER FOUR

I HAD BEEN LOOKING forward to a fun pre-nuptial evening even more than the wedding. Of course I wanted to have a lovely wedding. For our exchange of vows, I'd selected a reading that I thought embodied who Scoobie and I were together.

I didn't feel anxious. The wedding simply felt like adding a dot to an i. Scoobie and I were together with or without whatever George and Scoobie came up with for the ceremony.

Ramona's voice came from the front foyer of the B&B. "Jolie. I forgot my tape measure. Do you have one?"

Aunt Madge opened a kitchen drawer with one finger and pointed to it with her head, since she had confectioners' sugar on her hands.

I grabbed the cloth measure, the kind sewers like Aunt Madge used, and trotted through the swinging door toward the foyer. "What are you measuring?"

Michelle and Julia sat halfway up the stairs on the landing, in their matching blue, quilted bathrobes. At nine, Julia is the older of my two nieces, but seven-year-old Michelle is almost as tall as her sister.

The girls' eyes were wide as Ramona leaned over the banister, apparently trying to guess the distance to the floor below. She saw me and grinned. "I want to have a cascade of flowers from about this point on the stairs to the floor below."

I walked up several steps and tossed her the tape measure. "That sounds like a lot of trouble. For an evening, I mean."

She unfurled the tape and motioned that I should go down the steps to stand below her. "But you'll have the memories for a lifetime."

The girls giggled. I turned slightly as I went down the steps. "I can tell you're planning something."

Giggles turned to laughter, and Michelle clapped her hands. "It's such a big surprise!"

Julia put a finger to her lips. "And you'll never guess."

I kept my tone cheerful. "I just can't wait."

I kept walking and stood below Ramona. I mouthed, "What is it?"

She shrugged and mouthed, "Don't know." Then she said, "I'll hang onto the tape and you grab the end."

The ancient measuring tape has been wound and unwound so many times it's practically see-through in a couple of spots. It dangled limply, and I grabbed and extended it. "So, this is about sixty inches. I guess another couple of feet more to the floor."

"Measure that, would you?"

I used an index finger to mark on the wall the spot where the tape measure ended. She dropped it, and I fiddled with unfurling it so I could measure from the spot where it had hit sixty inches. *Not what I planned to be doing tonight.*

I felt a pang of guilt as Ramona moved down the steps to take over measuring. I cared only about the vows and spending time with friends, but Ramona was giving her best gifts – time and talent.

She took the measure from me and started from my finger. "Okay, another twenty-seven inches. Good eye."

I stepped back. "Don't suppose you'll tell me your plans."

Her bright pink, hooped earrings moved as she shook her head. "You'll love it."

Aunt Madge called from the kitchen. "Girls, time to frost."

Michelle clattered down the steps and burst into the kitchen. Julia traipsed slowly and stopped near me. "We might make a mess. With the icing."

I stared into her dark eyes and pretended to frown. "Do messes taste better or worse than perfect-looking cakes?"

She seemed to ponder this before slowly smiling. "They taste the same, silly."

I bent to hug her, and whispered, "Messes made from love. Go help frost the cakes."

Ramona rolled up the tape measure. "Your sister sure has raised good kids."

"Yep." I patted my slight baby bump. "I'm hoping it rubs off."

Car headlights in the B&B lot announced Scoobie and George. One of them honked. I opened the side door so they'd know we heard them. Then I realized the honk was likely to ensure we opened the door because they were hauling boxes from George's back seat.

I peered out, then turned to look at Ramona, open-mouthed. "You said simple decorations."

She grinned. "They are simple, I didn't say *few* decorations."

"Uh, okay."

"Really, Jolie, it's just that I packed the silk flowers carefully so they wouldn't get smushed."

My shoulders, which I had not realized were tense, loosened. "Good thinking." I stood back as she opened the screen door to let in the guys.

My first wedding had been a huge production. It was a beautiful day, despite the outcome a few years later, but I remembered how nervous I had been that some of the 200 details would not be perfect. This wedding, my *forever* wedding, would be a relaxing evening with family and friends.

Scoobie bounded up the stairs. "I expect union wages."

George called from behind him, "I'll take any pay."

"We ordered pizza," I said.

Scoobie stomped snow on the area rug by the door. He kicked off his shoes and turned to hold the door for George. With a grin, he sort of threw a kiss over his shoulder.

Ramona's usual airy-fairy tone was commanding. "The boxes marked 'kitchen' go in the great room. The ones with an F go in front of the fireplace in the living room that B&B guests use."

George muttered something about other F words as he strode past.

I stifled a giggle. "Thank you George. And be glad the girls are in the kitchen."

It took less than ten minutes for the boxes of silk flowers, vases, and tall candles to populate the floor in the great room. Ramona enlisted the eager Julia and Michelle to carry flowers, a few at a time, to different parts of the room.

She wouldn't let me help, noting the bride did not work on decorations.

"Excuses me," Scoobie said.

George grinned. "Trust me, you're just here as an ornament for the bride."

Ramona paid no attention to him, but Aunt Madge, Renée and I glowered at him. George wisely buried his face in a fragrant cider punch Harry handed him.

I grinned at Renée. She watched the girls hold silk flowers for Miss Piggy to smell. "I wish Andrew were here."

Renée's husband is a keep-to-himself kind of person. He's very protective of her and the girls, but is not one to spend much time at big social events.

"Too much snow falling," I volunteered.

She rolled her eyes.

Aunt Madge turned from the counter and held up one frosted cake for my inspection. "The girls decided on a Scooby Doo theme for this one."

I didn't know whether she bought the decorations or the girls brought them, but they definitely were good for a laugh.

Scoobie shook his head. "I have no idea why I've always had my name."

Aunt Madge looked at him thoughtfully. "I don't know, of course, but by the time you were in elementary school you were quite firm about keeping it."

He grabbed a punch and leaned on the counter. "Okay, I have a few memories of you when I was little, but how the heck would you know that?"

"A couple of my friends taught back then. Let's see, second and fourth grades, I think. They'd enlist me for various volunteer things."

"Cooking. I think sewing for school plays," Renée said.

"How come you know that and I don't?" I asked.

"Well...I guess by the time you'd have a lot of memories I had the B&B. Busy times."

That was sort of code for saying Uncle Gordon had died and she needed to earn a living. I blew her a kiss.

Ramona's voice came from near the back door. "Don't open that box, girls. It's the last thing I'll do tomorrow."

"You mean please, right?" Michelle asked.

Renée rolled her eyes and walked over to her daughters. "It's implied."

Ramona smiled. "Please."

"Baths in ten minutes, girls," Renée said.

I'd babysat for them enough that I knew complaints generally followed this statement, but since they were in Aunt Madge's house, they simply made faces.

Harry called from the stove. "I've made kid-size cider cups. Just a taste before bed, girls."

I watched him cater to them finding, as usual, it hard to imagine a time without him in Aunt Madge's life. Scoobie and I had suggested he invite his son's family, which included two favorite grandsons, to the

25

wedding. He said they already had plans to host a New Year's Eve party. Which, as Scoobie had told him with a grin, was our plan, too.

WITH THE GIRLS IN BED an hour later and Ramona done instructing Scoobie and George on where to place flowers or candles, we flung ourselves onto the loveseat or into upholstered chairs. Aunt Madge had her soft-casted ankle on an ottoman, but she continued to insist it felt as if it had never been broken.

She raised a glass of mulled wine to me. "I could beat you in a race any day."

"Well now, maybe," I said.

Scoobie and George, who don't drink, toasted Aunt Madge's cake decorating skills with cider. Scoobie asked, "What was that accident the police called you about?"

Aunt Madge sat up straighter. "Anyone we know?"

George shook his head. "An older man, Florida plates on the car. Not sure if he slid on the snow or had a seizure or what. He didn't hit the light pole all that hard."

"And the snow wasn't that bad. Was he conscious?" I asked.

"Not that I saw. Breathing on his own and all that. Looked like mostly banged up from the steering wheel."

Mr. Rogers yipped. He had carefully positioned himself near me, since he knows Aunt Madge will never give him any scraps.

I held up my cider. "You don't drink this."

The sound of light lapping came from the far end of the couch. Jazz daintily sipped the remnants of Harry's mulled wine.

I LAY IN BED TWO HOURS later feeling relaxed and happy. In keeping with tradition, Scoobie and I were in different beds, different houses. He said he would sleep at our bungalow to keep our pet skunk, Pebbles, company.

But I knew he also needed time to himself. When Scoobie and I met again three years ago, he often escaped into his poetry or traipsed solo along the boardwalk. As he has grown increasingly happy he's become better able to spend time with lots of people. In fact, anyone who worked with him at the hospital would consider him quiet but certainly sociable. Especially with kids.

Jazz snuggled against my neck, snoring softly.

"That's what you get for drinking wine," I whispered.

I closed my eyes. This had been one of the happiest nights of my life. And tomorrow would be even better.

CHAPTER FIVE

THE SNOW THAT FELL overnight meant that on New Year's Eve morning the Victorian-style B&B looked like a tourist photo for a Vermont ski resort, minus the mountains in the background. The roads were slick, but inside a fire burned in the guest living room, on the opposite side of the first floor foyer from Aunt Madge and Harry's great room and bedroom.

Silk flowers were piled on a loveseat in front of the fire, and Jazz sat atop them. I picked her up and slung her over my shoulder as we moved into the foyer. "Do you know what Ramona would do to you if she found you on that pile of ribbon and silk?"

She turned her head and swatted me in the back of mine.

"Nice. She'd swat you somewhere else."

I sat her on the floor and admired the ribbon that wound down the B&B's main staircase. Ramona's talent transformed the front hall and great room. Thankfully, she had interspersed her signature purple with a lot of white.

In the great room, one item was draped only in purple. The nearly life-sized portrait of our late, good friend Lance Wilson stood near the windows next to the sliding glass doors that faced the back yard. Lance sported a floral apron, supplied by Scoobie for Lance's use at the bake sale table at one of the food pantry fundraisers. Unknown to Lance when the photo was taken, George's hand behind him appeared to place a cupcake on Lance's head.

I started to tear up, but remembered I had on mascara and my sister would have a fit if it ran. I could hear her upstairs, helping Michelle and Julia blow-dry their hair.

My ivory dress was calf-length and tailored, with tiny beads sewn at the cuffs and neckline. Though more formal than a dinner dress, I hadn't bought it at a bridal shop. Aunt Madge had threaded a thin purple ribbon just under my breasts for an a-line effect. I thought she wanted to make sure my slightly round tummy wasn't too obvious. Not that the baby-to-be was a secret.

I would don the dress just before I walked down the stairs with Harry this evening. With my usual maladroitness, I would get toothpaste or coffee on it if I wore it even an hour earlier.

I had not seen Scoobie yet. Per her usual, Jazz had awakened me early, demanding food. At the girls' insistence, Scoobie and I were going to spend the day apart. Unless we decided we didn't want to.

My sister endorsed us staying apart, which was funny. Renée and Andrew met for a very early breakfast the morning of their wedding. Had she known, our mother would have been horrified. She thought Renée spent a long time getting her hair done.

My phone chirped and I pulled it from the pocket of my blue Dockers. Scoobie. I guess we hadn't said we would avoid talking before the wedding.

"Hello, my groom-to-be."

With no preamble, he asked, "Is Max over there?"

"No. Weren't you and George meeting him at Java Jolt at nine?"

"Yeah, we're here, he isn't. Have you ever known him to miss a muffin?"

Java Jolt is one of Max's favorite haunts. Like the prior operator, Megan gives Max pieces of broken muffins or other pastries.

"Do you think he thought you meant he should meet you at the B&B?"

"No. We had a couple talks to explain that couples often don't see each other before the ceremony."

George's voice came from somewhere near Scoobie. "Max thought it was stupid."

I could hear George and Scoobie talking quietly. I thought about options. "Scoobie."

He spoke into the phone again. "Yeah?"

"Harvest for All isn't open today. I'll call the grocery store."

"I guess we'll gulp our coffee and head over to his house."

"I'll let everybody here know to tell me if he calls them. I'll call you if he shows up at the B&B."

We disconnected, and I stayed seated on Aunt Madge's love seat, which had been pushed against the far wall to accommodate the twenty-five white chairs she rented. Max was a creature of habit. His usual routine did not include meeting Scoobie and George for muffins. Maybe he got confused.

I didn't know Max's regular schedule, or if he even had one beyond coffee at Java Jolt, visits to Harvest for All, and watching *Big Bang Theory*. Scoobie was probably more aware of where Max hung out, and he always said I should let go of things I couldn't control. I would make some calls, but I wouldn't worry about Max. Much.

BY THE TIME SCOOBIE called back, I had finished cutting up raw vegetables and Aunt Madge, at her insistence, had made several loaves of her cheddar cheese bread.

"Did you find him?"

Scoobie's tone seemed subdued. "No."

"Where are you?"

"At the hospital."

"I thought you didn't have to work...oh, you were looking for Max?"

"Yeah, and I may have found...can you come out here?"

Aunt Madge could hear Scoobie's voice, and shrugged at me.

"Um, sure. Are you okay?"

"More or less."

My stomach tightened and I leaned my back into the kitchen counter. This was not my excited husband-to-be, he of the dried pine needle wreaths. "I can be there in about fifteen minutes."

"Good, I'll see you...listen, can you bring Aunt Madge?"

"She can," Aunt Madge called to him.

Scoobie chuckled. "I see her hearing is as good as ever. Look, I'm okay. I just need both of you."

I hung up and stared at Aunt Madge, who had already taken off her apron. "He never sounds like that."

"He's okay. Maybe someone you know is in the ER."

"Jolie?" Renée had apparently come through the swinging door when Aunt Madge and I were paying attention to the call. "Everything all right?"

I glanced at her. "I think so. Scoobie went to the hospital to look for Max. He wants us to come over." When she started to say something, I added, "He says he's fine." *More or less.*

Renée is six years older than I am, and has always been very matter-of-fact. I could have told her the roof caved in at Ocean Alley's hospital and she would have approached the sink to finish putting the cut-up vegetables into plastic bags so we could take them to first responders.

"I'll finish that. The girls have their iPads."

A bark from the back yard reminded us of the high-spirited retrievers. Mister Rogers had his nose so close to the glass door that spots of condensation graced it. Miss Piggy head butted him so she would be closer to the opening.

Aunt Madge frowned. "Let me wipe their feet off while you go get your coat."

We were in the car in five minutes. I swallowed hard. Whatever my usually easygoing fiancé was up to, morning sickness wouldn't help.

CHAPTER SIX

AUNT MADGE AND I AREN'T big on idle chatter, so we said little on the short drive to Ocean Alley Hospital. Even at the shore we Jersey people are used to snow, so the streets had been cleared fairly well. Not so for all the driveways of the small bungalows and larger duplexes that lined our route. People were probably waiting for it to warm up a bit before they shoveled.

I felt a pang of guilt for not being more concerned about Max. What if he had been in the cold all night? I pushed the thought aside. Unless he were injured, he'd call Scoobie or the police. Scoobie had programmed the non-emergency number into Max's cell phone. He wouldn't have been on the street.

We had Aunt Madge's car, a bright red Taurus with its temporary handicapped sticker, so I parked near the ER entrance of the three-story hospital. "Wait until I come around to help you out."

She opened the passenger door. "Oh, sure. Let's have the pregnant woman on the ground rather than the old gal with a cast."

I couldn't help it. I giggled. "Let me at least help you onto the sidewalk."

I didn't have to. Scoobie hurried out the hospital door and had reached the car. "Hello ladies." He blew me a kiss.

That calmed me. He seemed more like himself.

Scoobie stepped off the curb into the parking space, and put a hand on Aunt Madge's bicep.

"It's easier to do it myself." When Scoobie continued to guide her, she added, "I forgot my cane. I can't beat you."

Scoobie grinned at me. "Beat me?" He seemed to read my expression. "It's okay. I'll tell you when we're inside."

We stomped our boots on the rubber mat inside the door, and Aunt Madge tapped her walking cast against the door frame to shake the snow off. She looked at Scoobie as she undid her scarf. "What's going on?"

He pointed to the nearly vacant waiting area. "Have a seat."

"Will we need it?" I asked.

"Probably not, but your aunt's a gimp."

His tone was light, but I knew something had really gotten to him. I slid out of my coat as I sat on the vinyl chair.

Scoobie sat and took a breath. His eyes moved between Aunt Madge and me. "So, I came here to check on Max. He hasn't been in. But I saw Harriet, you know, she works in the ER."

Aunt Madge and I both nodded. Harriet had brought me a pair of crutches one time when I made a hospital appearance.

"So, she looked kind of uncomfortable, and she asked me if I had any family here. When I told her no live ones I knew of, she frowned."

A voice over the public address system paged a doctor to go to the pediatric unit.

Scoobie continued. "Turns out, the guy they brought in, from that accident George went to last night, his name is O'Brien."

Aunt Madge sat up straighter. "Oh?"

Scoobie introduces himself with just the one name, so half the time I forget he's an O'Brien. It would be good to remember a husband's last name.

"His driver's license was from Florida and expired a couple years ago. They haven't been able to get a bead on him."

"Can George help?" I asked.

Scoobie sat up straighter and drew a deeper breath. "Probably only Aunt Madge."

"How old?" she asked.

"About sixty." Scoobie and she locked eyes for a moment, and then he looked at me. "Which would be roughly my father's age."

I blurted, "But you don't even know if he's alive."

"No kidding."

I flushed. "I'm sorry, I…"

"Not an 'I'm sorry' thing. I haven't seen him for almost twenty years." He looked at Aunt Madge again. "You'd be more likely to recognize him than I would. I don't even have a photo."

Aunt Madge stood. "I'm on it."

Scoobie rose more slowly, and nodded at me. "Why don't you stay here? He's got a lot of bruising, and a black eye from the accident. They told me he hasn't really been awake."

I nodded. As he and Aunt Madge moved away, I heard her ask if the man was badly injured. Scoobie shook his head and shrugged as he pulled out his hospital ID and they entered the ER's treatment area.

Several seconds went by before I even shifted in the uncomfortable seat. I had seen Scoobie's mother briefly a couple of years ago, perhaps the only truly evil person I'd encountered. Sure, I'd met a couple of murderers. But her neglect of Scoobie, and his occasional childhood 'accidents,' were deliberate and mean. I felt no sorrow when she was gone.

Aunt Madge had once said Scoobie and books raised Scoobie. No one seemed to know where his father had gone. Scoobie had given me only a broad-brush background.

When my parents sent me to live with Aunt Madge during junior year, I was mad at everyone. Scoobie made me laugh. Eventually there were hints of his mother's behavior, but he maintained a class clown demeanor. He also reminded me from time to time that I and any problems I had were not the center of the universe. He was a good friend and a reality check.

And then I went back to Lakewood for my senior year, and we'd lost touch until three years ago. It took a while for us to click romantically. At least for me. Scoobie says he waited for me to catch up.

My eyes teared. He was in pain when we were in high school, and I hadn't really known. Now he might be again, and he turned to Aunt Madge. *Oh, damn. Mascara.*

I pulled a tissue from my coat pocket and blotted my eyes. I should never have put on the eye makeup so early. *Why are you thinking of eye makeup?!* Because, at this minute, I felt powerless to help Scoobie. For the hundredth time, my faith was in Aunt Madge.

The door to the patient area opened, and a woman in pink scrubs stuck her head out, scanning the waiting room. Harriet. "Jolie? Come on back."

I stood, my heart beating fast and my stomach roiling. At least ER rooms had plastic barf dishes.

"Hey, Harriet. Thanks for helping Scoobie."

I would describe her smile as pained.

"Not sure he thinks so, but sometimes it's better to know than not know."

I followed her behind a curtain and saw Aunt Madge with her arm around Scoobie's shoulder. He was clear-eyed, but solemn.

I took in the equipment that beeped and showed lines monitoring the man's vital signs before looking at the person on the gurney. Even with a swollen face, the shape of the head and mouth was like Scoobie's. No doubt in my mind. Scoobie had found his father, whether he wanted to or not.

CHAPTER SEVEN

AS HARRIET CHECKED THE flow of an IV, Aunt Madge asked, "Why is he still in the emergency room?"

"Partially because we have lower staff levels on the floors, since it's the New Year's holiday. More people to monitor him in here."

That made sense, though the gurney the man had been on for at least twelve hours didn't look too comfortable.

Harriet smiled at Scoobie as she closed the orange curtain behind her. Before I could say a word to Scoobie, the curtain swished open with a squeak.

Sergeant Morehouse looked at each of us in turn, his glance landing on me. "Like I always say, you sure know how to pick 'em."

Scoobie smiled weakly. "If you mean me, I'm insulted."

Morehouse, with his close-cropped hair and wearing the polyester pants that are his version of a uniform, gave a grim smile. "I suppose no insults on your wedding day. Or night, whatever the hell you're doin'. Know him?"

Aunt Madge spoke. "I believe this is Terence O'Brien. I knew him before Adam was born. Scoobie."

Scoobie met my eyes and we smiled. Aunt Madge had always called him by his given name. She occasionally relapses.

She continued. "Terence Adam O'Brien."

Scoobie pulled back so he could look at her directly. "You have *got* to be kidding. You can't ever call me Adam again."

Several thoughts went through my head. How could a person not know their father's middle name? How did Aunt Madge know it? Why hadn't she ever told Scoobie? Or maybe she assumed he knew. Or that he didn't care.

The man on the gurney stirred, but it seemed more from restlessness than awareness. He had, as Scoobie said, a major black eye. Swelling on his left cheek likely came from hitting the steering wheel. Bruising covered the cheek and went down his neck. He wore a light blue hospital gown and two IVs flowed into him. The person on the stretcher appeared more vulnerable old man than the monster Scoobie's mother had often described to him.

I looked at Morehouse. "Do you know what happened to him?"

He shook his head. "Only from the time of his accident. Hospital thinks he passed out, probably why he hit the light pole. Maybe a heart attack. They been treatin' him for one, and wanna do more tests. Hope whatever they do helps him wake up some more."

"And he was alone?"

Morehouse studied me. "Aren't you getting married tonight?"

"Doesn't impair my thinking."

Scoobie began, "Jolie...Oh hell, I don't know what I want to know."

I wasn't sure he'd want a big hug in front of Morehouse, so I tried to make my look one of understanding and love.

Morehouse pulled a thin notebook from the pocket of his plaid sport coat. "So, you obviously didn't know he was comin', and you hadn't talked to him recently."

Scoobie began, "Right on both..."

I broke in "Hey."

The three of them looked at me. Aunt Madge asked, "What is it? Do you feel okay?"

"Yes." I frowned in Morehouse's direction. "I can't be sure, but he looks a little like a man who ate in the diner last night." I studied at Scoobie's father more closely. "Or maybe not. I guess not."

Morehouse's stare in my direction conveyed irritation. "All we know is that he may have had someone with him. Or maybe a guy seen walking away wasn't with him."

"What did the person look like?" Aunt Madge asked.

He glanced at his notes. "Short, but not a kid. Red hat with some kind of decoration on top."

I HAD A MISSION. If Max had been in the car or nearby when Scoobie's father had a meeting with a lamppost, Max saw it and was scared. When scared, Max stayed in his house or found Scoobie. Only he hadn't done either.

I had little time. Guests would arrive at nine P.M., and I had no intention of spending the afternoon scouring town for Max. I would look for an hour. After that I'd have exhausted all my ideas.

Scoobie and Aunt Madge stayed at the hospital, though Scoobie said he would drive them both back to the B&B very soon.

I pulled into Steele Appraisals, which was in Harry's former home, and climbed the steps. I briefly took note of his latest repairs, replacing rotted trim around windows on the front porch, and wondered if he would ever be done restoring his grandparents' old place.

Since I hadn't planned on working, I didn't have my keys. I pounded on the door.

Harry's rapid footsteps said I had alarmed him. He opened the door, his face a question mark. "Madge?"

"Oh, God, Harry, she's fine. I'm sorry." I strode into the foyer. "You've been around town today, have you seen Max?"

"No." He led me toward the room on the right that served as the office. "You think something's wrong?"

I told him about the day's events, and he whistled. "And on your wedding day. But no, I haven't seen him. I headed to the courthouse to look up some properties before it closed at noon."

Harry was doing work I would normally have handled. If a couple of recent requests for appraisals hadn't come in, he'd be at the B&B helping us get ready for the wedding. Or maybe he preferred work here to the confusion that would soon reign at the Cozy Corner.

"Scoobie went by his house, and Megan's been telling people at Java Jolt to keep an eye out for him. I wish I hadn't closed Harvest for All for New Year's Eve. Half the people who go in there would know him."

I followed Harry into our joint office and plopped on a chair in front of his desk.

Harry sat down and tapped on his desk with a pen. "And Reverend Jamison's gone, so no one could let him into the pantry?"

"Yes, and his secretary..." I stopped. "I think Max knows where the spare key is hidden."

"You want me to go with you?"

I rose from my chair. "If something scared him, it should be just me."

CHURCHES STRIKE ME AS eerily quiet when you're alone in them, even if you're in the church basement. I closed the door that led to the street and made for the food pantry down the hall.

As usual, the door was locked when we weren't open, so I unlocked it and flipped on the light. From a shelf near the back came a gasp.

"Max?" He must have been on the floor, because I heard him bump against a shelf at the end of an aisle as he stood.

"I only ate a little. Just some peanut butter and bread. Only a little." He had reached the end of the aisle and faced me.

I went behind the counter and hugged him briefly, careful not to knock off his antler hat. "Max, you can have any food you need. We've been so worried about you."

As if I'd wound up a key on his back, he began to pace. "It was all my fault. My fault."

"What? Max, even if you did something, accidents happen." As I said the words, my brain focused better. Max had left Newhart's Diner at about the same time as the man I now knew was Scoobie's father. "Oh, you think you caused the car to hit the utility pole? That's not what happened."

"French fries at Burger King. Burger King. Straight home, no accident."

It's a challenge to figure out Max's thought process. It seemed he had stopped for French fries and thought if he had not, somehow the car would not have hit the pole.

"Max, you were just in the wrong place at the wrong time. It wasn't your fault."

"Against the light. Scoobie said never to cross against the light."

I leaned on the counter. Sometimes I'm so tired I can't stand it, a weariness that's supposed to end by the start of my second trimester. "Max, they think the man had a heart attack."

He stopped and faced me. "Should I do CPR? CPR?"

I smiled. "He's being well taken care of in the hospital. You didn't do anything wrong."

"Jaywalking. Scoobie said I can get a ticket for walking. Jaywalking."

I straightened my shoulders. "You know how on Fourth of July everyone goes to the beach to watch the fireworks? Hundreds and hundreds of people cross the street when it's over. Do you understand? They all jaywalk."

"Jaywalking."

"Max, Scoobie helps you learn to be safe. Remember, same as Josh did."

Josh, another veteran who had mostly lived on the streets, had essentially been Max's caregiver before he left town. When Max met Scoobie and me, all of us, it was the luckiest day of his life.

"Flowers. We could take flowers to the hospital."

I glanced around the room for a moment. I had often stood in the same spot, reading the grocery lists of local residents and people passing through town who knew the pantry would always give them something, even if we didn't have much.

"I'll tell you what. We'll have flowers at Aunt Madge's for the wedding. Tomorrow, not tonight, you can take some to the hospital. If the man is still there. Maybe he'll be better."

Probably not better, if he had a heart attack.

"Is Scoobie mad? Mad at me?"

"Oh, damn." I took my mobile phone from my jacket pocket. "No, he's not mad. I have to call and tell him I found you. Then we'll go see him at the Cozy Corner."

His frown lifted. "I'll clean up my mess. My mess."

I watched him retreat to the spot where he'd been hiding as I listened to Scoobie's phone ring.

A couple hours ago we'd thought our biggest challenge was finding our brain-injured friend. Now Scoobie's father had essentially found us. I doubted that Scoobie would want his absent father being an active grandfather, but I'd been surprised by a lot of people lately. Especially the little one in my tummy.

CHAPTER EIGHT

I TOOK MAX BACK TO the Cozy Corner. Scoobie could help him understand that Max crossing the street had nothing to do with the accident. Max always took Scoobie's advice as if it came from Mount Sinai. When I'd called him to say I'd found Max, Scoobie said he'd be home soon.

But Aunt Madge and Scoobie were not back. I offered him tea, which he refused, and then guided Max to sit by the sliding door to look at the snow, now indented with paw prints.

George and Renée drank coffee at the oak table as Michelle and Julia tried to show George that Jazz was good friends with Mister Rogers and Miss Piggy. Jazz disagreed.

I lifted Jazz off the fridge as Max, saying nothing, watched the antics from across the room. "Girls, Aunt Madge doesn't want a cat on top of the fridge. It's not sanitary."

Julia looked at me with all the patience a nine-year-old can muster. "She must go up there a lot. She did it really fast."

"Is she trying to get away from Miss Piggy and Mister Rogers?" Michelle asked.

My sister tried to quell a laugh. "Not the dogs, no. Why don't you get ready to make a snow man?"

"Isn't it snow people?" George asked, as the kitchen door to the breakfast room swung shut behind the girls.

"Shut up, George," Renée and I said.

"Jeez. Usually I don't get stereo." He focused on me. "You saw Scoobie's old man?"

I nodded, and led the dogs to the sliding glass door so they could romp in the snow. "Aunt Madge was certain, and Scoobie looks a lot like him."

George shook his head. "Why in the hell did he have to show up last night?"

I sat at the oak table with Renée and George and met his eyes. "Did you know Scoobie's father before he left?"

George shook his head. "I'm a year older than you two, remember? In middle school that was a big difference."

Renée tilted her head to listen to her girls' voices drifting down the stairs. Apparently satisfied with what she heard, she addressed George. "I remember meeting Scoobie at Christmas the year Jolie lived here, but not you."

George looked into his mug and back at her. "Scoobie and I didn't get to be good friends until I came back from college."

I knew that was code for attending AA together.

"It's hard to tell with his face so banged up, but I keep wondering if he was a man I saw at Newhart's last night. He was there with...oh my." The child came to mind. Or the back of the kid's head, anyway.

I stood. "Scoobie's still with Aunt Madge at the hospital. I have to call them."

"Jolie," Renée began.

"Where are you...?" George started.

I reached the breakfast area before I dialed Scoobie's mobile phone.

His singsong voice greeted me. "Hi, love of my life and chief troublemaker."

"Where are you?"

"Aunt Madge and I are just leaving the hospital. What's up?"

"In Newhart's last night. If the man I saw talking to Elmira was your father, he had a kid with him."

"Let me pull over."

"What is it?" Aunt Madge asked.

"I'm putting you on speaker," Scoobie said. He repeated to Aunt Madge what I had just told him.

I frowned. "I don't know if Elmira knew him or was just talking to him."

"A boy," Scoobie said. "How old?"

"I only saw the back of his head. I'd guess ten or so. Maybe that means your father was visiting someone here, that people could look for him."

"I'm referring to him as 'the absent Terence.' That's TAT, and I'm debating whether I should be noble or practice tit-for-tat."

I smiled. "I'll try to remember. And do what you want."

George opened the swinging door partway and stuck his head into the breakfast room. "What did the kid look like?"

"George, I'm talking to Scoobie!"

He came into the breakfast room. "Put me on speaker."

I ignored him.

Renée joined us. "A child? The man's child?"

The thought had occurred to me, but the kid seemed more the age of a grandchild. Scoobie would be floored if he learned his father had a second family. What kinds of relationships would those people expect to have with us? How would we handle that? I didn't know how I felt about it, and couldn't imagine Scoobie's thoughts.

Without asking, George took the mobile phone from my hand. He held up one finger, silencing me. Since Renée stood next to me, I decided not to swat at the phone.

"So, Scoob. I got there not long after your old man hit that pole. I didn't see any kid."

My anger faded. I'd forgotten George took photos at the accident scene last night. "Push the speaker."

George did, and Scoobie said, "Jolie, you better talk to Morehouse again. You weren't sure the man you saw was my father…"

"I'm still not, but maybe."

George, how about you see if Arnie Newhart will let you look at his security camera video?"

"I should make that call, George," Aunt Madge said. "He'll think you're looking for a story."

George scowled, but said, "It's been a while since I worked at the paper, but you may be right."

She continued, "Scoobie, drop me at Newhart's. Jolie, where were they sitting?"

"Not far from the entry door." I knitted my brow in concentration. "Scoobie and I were in that back booth we like. His father, uh, TAT, faced me. Scoobie's back was to him."

Aunt Madge spoke again. "We're driving again. You need to focus on the wedding. Don't worry about any of this."

George's face brightened. "I'll call Elmira to find out if she actually knows him."

"See you soon." Scoobie hung up.

Renée looked at me. "Madge is right. Leave this to others."

"I only care if a little kid is sitting somewhere waiting for that old man to come back."

GEORGE LEFT, AND RENÉE decided that she needed to keep the girls away from the conversation about Scoobie's father. She went outside to help with what Michelle said would be a snow family.

I felt so tired I could have slept on the floor, but I also wanted to talk to Max. I glanced at the clock. Nearly one P.M. Ramona would get off work at the Purple Cow Office Supply Store at three, and planned to come over to finish decorations. She would probably be willing to keep Max busy while I took a nap.

I sat next to Max on the loveseat in the great room. "You feeling better?"

His mouth drooped and shoulders slumped. Sometimes it's easy to forget Max is probably close to forty. "I should have helped the man."

"You aren't a doctor, Max. Scoobie will be here in a bit. He can let you know the man is doing okay."

He nodded.

"Let's see what's on TV in the guests' living room."

"Soap operas and game shows. Game shows, but not *Jeopardy*. *Jeopardy*. Today is the finals day on *Jeopardy*."

I smiled. "Okay, you can wait 'til it comes on. Before then you can vacuum in the front hall for me."

He straightened. "Vacuuming! I love to vacuum."

I nodded. "I do have one quick question."

"What question? A question about a question? In *Jeopardy* you ask questions."

I felt more tired by the moment. "Remember when you were leaving the restaurant last night, a nice man talked to you for a moment?"

"He's a vet. A Veteran of Foreign Wars."

That floored me. "You know him?"

"He had a hat."

"Ah. I get it. So, did the boy with him have a hat?"

"Florida Panthers ski cap. No skiing in Florida. Panthers."

I grinned broadly. "You are so smart, Max."

He sobered. "I used to be."

"So, the boy. Do you think he was local? From Ocean Alley?"

"Don't know him. Know him. Ask Megan. Megan knows everybody. Everybody."

"Good idea. I will. In the meantime, I want to call Sergeant Morehouse."

"Am I in trouble for leaving? For leaving?"

"No, of course not. I want to see if, uh, he knows the boy."

"Sergeant Morehouse has nephews. Nephews. They sell Christmas trees with him. Trees."

I'd never met the two nephews, but another officer had once told me he was great with them. "Good point, maybe they'll know. Come on, let's get out the vacuum."

After eating some of the celery we'd cut up for tonight, I lay down on the loveseat and called Morehouse.

"How come you're callin' me just hours before your wedding?"

"Max was the person who left the accident scene."

Two beats of silence, then Morehouse sighed. "I probably ought to talk to Max."

"You know how he is. We'd have to pick him off the floor. He didn't see anything, and his only concern is that he jaywalked and maybe the man swerved to avoid him."

"Did he talk to the guy?"

"No." I didn't actually know this, but since Max had left, I thought not. "But that's not actually why I'm calling." I relayed the information about a child being with Mr. O'Brien in Newhart's. I almost called the man TAT.

"You need to take a break. It's your wedding."

"So, Aunt Madge is on it. She's going to see if Arnie could get at his security videos."

Morehouse swore and hung up in his traditional manner. No goodbye. I debated calling him back to tell him about the VFW hat. He'd probably just hang up on me again.

LUNCH WAS SUPPOSED TO have been a quiet 'girls' meal' with Aunt Madge, Renée, Julia, Michelle, and me. Instead, George and Scoobie joined us. Harry said he wanted to finish some paperwork so he'd be appraisal-free for the wedding. I thought he was avoiding the day's hubbub. Who could blame him?

Scoobie squirted mustard on a slice of multigrain bread and added lettuce and two slices of cheese. "So, the hospital explained that they were going to finish some tests and move the patient to a room near ICU."

Julia and Michelle had no idea who we were taking about, per Renée's preference. I could tell Julia understood that we were using evasive terms, but she probably figured she had a better chance of staying at the table if she didn't ask. She listened to see what she could pick up.

Julia gestured toward Scoobie with a slice of apple. "So, do you have to go do an x-ray for somebody?"

Scoobie shook his head. "Nope. It's someone I know, so my friends at the hospital let me know they're taking good care of him."

Which is more than he did for you.

Michelle came out of a daydream. "Is your friend coming to the wedding?"

"Nope, but I'll visit him soon."

The girls looked at me.

"Me, too," I said.

Renée broke in before they could ask more questions. "Ramona put some extra silk flowers on the floor in the foyer closet. You can put a couple on the snow people when you finish eating."

They were done in a trice, and Renée left the room to shepherd them into coats and boots. She turned at the swinging door and mouthed, "Tell me later."

I grinned and mouthed, "Thank you."

Scoobie saluted her.

As the door swung shut, Aunt Madge asked, "Where are we?"

Scoobie straightened his shoulders. "If this wasn't about to be the best day of my life, I'd say in hell." He adopted a clown-sized grin. "But since it is the best day, I'll just say I'm in a confused state that I'm going to ignore for a day."

George finished chewing a Kosher dill pickle, and swallowed. "You want to hear what Elmira said, or wait 'til after the wedding?"

"Did she talk to him?" Scoobie asked.

"In a manner of speaking. He stopped her, seemed to remember her from before he left."

"And...?" I asked.

"And nothing. Said he was in town again, and would see her around. She said the boy looked half - asleep, hadn't finished his food."

Scoobie frowned. "Must have been someone else with them. He had to drop the kid somewhere before the accident."

"That makes sense," Aunt Madge said. "And it makes me feel better about the child to think that way."

So why isn't anyone looking for The Absent Terence O'Brien?

CHAPTER NINE

A NEW YEAR, A NEW LIFE. Fifteen years I'd known Scoobie, admittedly with a twelve-year lapse of contact. Our upcoming commitment to spend a lifetime together would take about five minutes.

Harry and I stood in the breakfast room as conversation ebbed in the great room. Aunt Madge had just said, "Excuse me," which quieted the room.

I whispered, "Harry, do you have your mobile phone turned on?"

"I do, and I'll place it in Scoobie's pocket when we get up there."

I thought about saying hello to my parents again, but if my mother had questions I'd have a hard time getting off the phone.

Aunt Madge's voice came again. "Everyone comfortable?"

A few muted replies reached us, and I figured most people nodded.

"Jolie and Scoobie didn't want traditional music, so they will be serenaded by two young ladies here."

Renée added. "For those who don't know them, these are Jolie's nieces, Michelle and Julia."

I could envision them in their deep blue, floor-length dresses. Renée had told me they really wanted to be flower girls – actually, Julia had said junior bridesmaid – but when Renée told them nothing would be 'that formal,' she had also promised they could wear long dresses.

The song surprised me.

Julia's voice, initially tremulous, gained strength. "Aunt Jolie and Scoobie…"

"Do we call him Uncle Scoobie now?" Michelle asked.

Harry put his hand over his mouth to keep from laughing out loud. I started to tear up.

George spoke, "Just Scoobie."

"How do you know?" Michelle asked.

"He hates titles," George said, and several people laughed.

Scoobie spoke, and I could almost see his smile. "Just Scoobie."

Julia's tone was strict. "Michelle, you're getting off-topic again."

The room exploded, and I laughed so hard I had to lean on Harry.

We composed ourselves as the room calmed. Harry whispered, "Use my handkerchief. You're mascara's running."

"Nuts." I took it and dabbed under my eyes.

Julia spoke again. "Because all kinds of people come into the food pantry and Aunt Jolie and Scoobie help everybody, we have a special song to sing." She paused, "Okay Dad, now."

Andrew must have turned on a CD, because instrumental music I could not immediately place began to play.

After about ten seconds, Michelle and Julia began to sing. "It's a world of laughter a world of tears, a world of hopes and a world of fears. There's so much that we share that it's time we're aware…"

"Oh, Harry, listen!"

He grinned broadly. "I'm happy to, but I think we're also supposed to make our entrance."

The door to the great room opened, revealing our friend Bill Oliver. He wore a tux with tails, and bowed.

This could be a more formal wedding than Scoobie and I planned.

Two voices warbled as we walked into the transformed great room. "It's a small world after all, it's a small world after all."

My eyes swept the room. In the half-hour Renée and I had spent getting me dressed upstairs, the room had been further transformed. Four large vases of flowers sat near the rows of guest chairs, two by the last row and two near Scoobie, who wore a gray tux and a rose boutonniere. Aunt Madge stood across from him, fulfilling her matron of honor duties in part by not trekking in front of me sporting her walking cast.

The chairs had been switched to face the windows. The night sky blinked into the room via stars that twinkled behind a white wicker arch. Chairs were now arranged in front of the windows. Scoobie and I would be wed beneath a traditional wedding arbor. *Where did that come from?*

As I looked at the broad smile on my soon-to-be husband's face, I realized my efforts to have a low-key wedding had been so misplaced. This would be fun!

As Harry and I strode the sixty or so feet toward Scoobie, I took in the guests. Most I had expected. Megan and her teenage daughter Alicia – when did she get so grown-up? – had broad smiles. Alicia gave me a small wave.

Dr. Welby, the most gregarious member of the Harvest for All Volunteer Committee, sat with two other members – the energetic Aretha and the local librarian, Daphne. Daphne's broad grin probably reflected memories of Scoobie's continual teasing to get her to let him take out more books than allowed.

Ramona's boss, Roland, had been invited in part because we like him and in part because he puts up with me a lot when I bug Ramona at the store. His wife, Nancy, I didn't know well, only that she was kind.

Father Teehan pointed a camera at us, probably to prove to Reverend Jamison that the wedding had been real. Sergeant Morehouse wore a dark wool suit and looked nothing like the polyester-clad police officer we usually dealt with. He smiled broadly, also something different.

A quick glance around the room showed Max in the last row, next to Mr. Markle. The grocer leaned over to say something to him. Probably something like "don't bolt."

The girls had finished their rendition of "It's a Small World After All" and were taking seats with Renée and Andrew. Julia stood primly, and Michelle seemed ready to burst with excitement.

Ramona was crying, of course, as Jennifer Stenner, another high school friend, dug in her purse to find a tissue for her. Mister Rogers had been stationed next to Scoobie, but he dashed to Ramona, licked her hand, and ran back to resume a regal pose next to Miss Piggy.

Only then did I realize the dogs had on bibs fashioned to look like tuxedos. A further look showed Jazz had climbed to the top of the arbor, well above where she could be easily reached. No doubt she judged her perch even better than the fridge. She stared at me, nonplussed.

By now all the guest were a blur of pastels, navy blues, and dark suits. I rubbed a finger under each eye to wipe away tears.

We got to Scoobie. Harry patted me on the arm and disengaged my vise-like grip on his elbow. "Behave yourself."

George and Aunt Madge both did something like a chortle. I took in her elegant, deep red dress and the joy in her expression.

Scoobie and I locked eyes. He grinned. "I knew you'd like it all."

I whispered, "It's lovely." I started to lean forward to kiss him, and pulled back. "Oops."

He took my hand and we both faced George. I'd never seen him in a black suit and a white, collared shirt. If he hadn't had red dolphins and light blue crabs on his dark blue tie I might not have known him.

George looked from Scoobie to me and back to Scoobie. "Whew."

Titters from Julia and Michelle, and someone in a kind of warbly voice said, "About time."

George held a black leather folder opened like a book. He could read his script without fumbling with papers. "Okay, on behalf of Jolie and Scoobie, let me welcome you to the first day of the rest of their lives."

For a moment I thought he was being flippant, but his earnestness made that unlikely.

"They have asked me to read some favorite passages. If you've known Scoobie for a while, you may remember that he used to take the book *The Prophet*, by Khalil Gibran, out of the library constantly."

Our librarian friend, Daphne, laughed, then said, "Sorry."

George grinned at her. "Trust me, sometimes he read me parts of it." George sombered. "From *The Prophet*."

> *Let there be spaces in your togetherness,*
> *And let the winds of the heavens dance between you.*
> *Love one another but make not a bond of love:*
> *Let it rather be a moving sea between the shores of your souls.*
> *Fill each other's cup but drink not from one cup.*
> *Give one another of your bread but eat not from the same loaf.*
> *Sing and dance together and be joyous.*

Renée gave a loud sniff.

George grinned at me. I didn't look at Scoobie. I'd never told him that when I first returned to Ocean Alley, I bought the library a new copy of *The Prophet*. I did it so Scoobie could keep renewing the library copy. I hoped Daphne would continue to keep my secret.

"Now, Jolie," George said, "has picked a reading from "Friendship," by Judy Bielicki.

> *It is often said that it is love that makes the world go round. However, without doubt, it is friendship which keeps our spinning existence on an even keel.*
>
> *True friendship provides so many of the essentials for a happy life -- it is the foundation on which to build an enduring relationship, it is the mortar which bonds us together in harmony, and it is the calm, warm protection we sometimes need when the world outside seems cold and chaotic.*
>
> *True friendship holds a mirror to our foibles and failings, without destroying our sense of worthiness.*
>
> *True friendship nurtures our hopes, supports us in our disappointments, and encourages us to grow to our best potential.*

George looked from Scoobie to me. "Jolie and Scoobie didn't want the other to know their selections before the ceremony. When I read them, it made it clear how important their friendship has been. So I would add Elbert Hubbard's quote. 'A friend is someone who knows all about you and still loves you.'"

I stole a look at Scoobie. His serious expression surprised me. George seemed disconcerted, too, because he moved quickly to the vows.

"And now, for the reason we are here tonight. Or I should say, this morning." He smiled at both of us.

"Do you, Jolie Gentil, take Scoobie O'Brien as your lawfully wedded husband?"

"I do."

George, in his role as best man, took my simple wedding band from his pocket and handed it to Scoobie. I held out my left hand. Scoobie easily slid the ring on my finger, and winked at me.

I felt myself redden, and my smile grew almost ridiculously wide.

"Do you, Scoobie O'Brien, take Jolie Gentil as your lawfully wedded wife?"

"With every fiber of my being."

Polite titters and one guffaw came from the attendees.

Aunt Madge had worn the band I planned to give Scoobie on one of her fingers. As she passed it to me, my hands shook slightly and I dropped it.

Jazz streaked from the top of the arbor before the ring hit the floor. She landed on the ring and slid about six feet with it under one claw.

Behaved though they could be on occasion, the launched ring was too much for Mister Rogers and Miss Piggy. Intent on her prize, Jazz gave Mister Rogers time to land on her. As was her habit, Miss Piggy head-butted his rump.

Exclamations of "oh my" and "get her!" filled the room as chairs scraped back.

Morehouse had been on the end of an aisle, and he tried to reach under Mister Rogers to grab Jazz. She wriggled out from under Mister Rogers and, ring now in her mouth, headed for the loveseat against the far wall.

Aunt Madge's voice rang through the room. "Jazz Gentil. You stop right this minute."

The dogs, used to obeying anything that sounded like a possible Aunt Madge command, froze. To my surprise, Jazz also stopped abruptly. She took one quick look over her shoulder at Aunt Madge, dropped the ring, and dashed under the loveseat.

Silence reigned for perhaps two beats. If Scoobie hadn't sat on the floor to laugh, probably the ensuing eruption would have quieted faster.

The dogs took Scoobie's seat on the floor as permission to climb on him, and even Aunt Madge leaned on George because she laughed so hard.

Morehouse stood from where he'd been bending over to pick up the ring, and shook a finger at me. I took in the room full of family and friends and burst into tears.

Happy tears that turned to laughter, but they were enough to quiet the room. Scoobie scrambled to his feet. "It's okay, honey."

I doubled over, holding my sides. When I finally stood, I saw a room of shocked attendees. I wiped the mascara now streaming down my face and managed to say, "Come on. It was funny."

Morehouse held out the ring and Scoobie took it. "I'm not gonna put this on you, but you can hold onto it better than your bride."

George's voice rose. "Okay, take two on the exchange of vows thing."

That brought more laughter, and I watched Harry and Andrew upright a couple of chairs that had flipped over as guests stood to watch the entertainment.

Scoobie and I faced George again. He leaned down and whispered, "Wipe your nose."

Scoobie had a handkerchief out in a flash, and I daintily, or so I thought, dabbed my cheeks and then nose.

George cleared his throat. "Do you, Scoobie O'Brien, take Jolie Gentil as your lawfully wedded wife?"

"With even more fibers of my being." He grinned broadly as he handed me his ring, and whispered, "Need any help?"

I shook my head, afraid I would cry again if I said anything. I took his extended hand and slipped the wedding band on the third finger of his left hand.

George's voice kind of croaked. "I now pronounce you husband and wife. You may now kiss the bride."

Scoobie and I leaned into each other. *We should have practiced the kind of kiss we wanted.*

I started to giggle and he whispered "dork" before his lips found mine. His left arm reached to my back below my shoulder blades and I latched onto his waist with my arm.

Okay, no tongue in front of a crowd.

Short and delicious. Those words played in my head for a fraction of a second before we seemed to simultaneously become aware of applause and a couple of hoots.

My cheeks burned as I smiled at my husband. Scoobie's goofy grin was plastered in the middle of a blushing face. "We did it," he said.

"Yes, we did."

My mother's voice emanated from Scoobie's pocket. "Jolie, what caused all that ruckus? Pick up!"

Julia and Michelle had wrapped themselves around me, so Harry grabbed my shoulder to keep me from tumbling backwards.

Scoobie reached into his pocket as Aunt Madge grabbed him in a proverbial bear hug.

Louder this time, "Jolie!"

Scoobie hugged Aunt Madge and handed me the phone.

"Hi Mom. Did you hear it all?"

"We did, Hon. When your Dad stops sniveling he'll tell you how happy we are for you."

Leave it to Mom to characterize tears of joy as sniveling.

Renée took the phone from my hand and held it to her ear. "Mom. Jolie's being swamped. I'll carry you around so you can hear everyone congratulate her and Scoobie."

For a hectic two minutes every guest came up to us with a congratulatory hug or peck on the cheek. Only a couple of people separated me from Aunt Madge, but each time one moved away another stepped forward. Our eyes met and she blew me a kiss.

Julia stepped forward and handed me a small nosegay. "You didn't want to carry flowers," she began.

"Because we know I would have dropped them."

"You didn't look nervous," she continued. "But later you have to throw these." She crooked a finger so I would lean over, and then whispered, "Michelle and me think Ramona and George should get married."

A few droplets flew by as, behind me, George choked on something liquid.

I took the yellow-blossomed nosegay and kept a solemn expression. "I'm sure they have lots of years to be friends."

Michelle crowded us. "Yes, but..."

Renée interrupted. "Come on girls. We have that other surprise to set up."

My eyes met my sister's. She smiled and shook her head slightly. Apparently whatever the surprise, I didn't need to worry about something like champagne-filled balloons.

Harry had hustled to the kitchen area to set up a punch table, and Aunt Madge and I could finally embrace.

"I can't believe you made the dogs tuxes."

She shrugged. "I had one for Jazz, but I didn't really expect to get it on her."

"Did you say 'It's about time?' I couldn't tell if it was a man or a woman."

She frowned. "Maybe I blitzed it out, but I don't remember anyone saying it."

"You know, right when Scoobie and I faced George."

Megan called from twenty feet away. "Smile you two."

Aunt Madge and I faced her. As I smiled my eyes met those in Lance Wilson's large portrait. I must have missed my oldest friend even more than I thought.

CHAPTER TEN

AFTER OUR BUBBLY CIDER toast I noted that Max had positioned himself as far from everyone as possible, near the sliding glass door. People weren't ignoring him, but he's not the easiest person to strike up a conversation with.

I put the cider on the drink table, took a ginger ale and orange juice punch from Harry, and tilted my head toward Max.

"I can head over there," he said.

I shook my head. "I haven't talked to him yet." I moved toward Max, catching Morehouse's eye as I moved toward the door. Morehouse winked at me. That was a first.

Max stared into the back yard. I spoke softly. "Did you like the ceremony?"

He turned partway. "Do you think the dogs want to come in? Come in?"

"Maybe in a few minutes. Did you want to go out?"

He frowned slightly.

"Or would you like to go in a room with fewer people?"

"Fewer people." He met my gaze. "Lots of people here, lots of people."

"Come on, let's go into the room with the fireplace. You can escort me."

"Escort. Harry escorted you."

"Yep, now you can."

Max looked happier than when Aunt Madge gave him all the leftover Halloween candy last year.

I linked my arm through his elbow and we walked to the breakfast room and then across the foyer, into the guest living room.

Ramona and Bill Oliver sat in a grouping of chairs on the far end of the large room, but no one sat on the loveseat in front of the fire. Ramona smiled and Bill nodded. They resumed their conversation.

"Do you like to watch the fire, Max?"

He sat on the deep brown loveseat and relaxed into it. "Fire is bright. Bright fire."

I sat next to him, but on the edge of the seat, and handed him the ginger ale punch. "It's very pretty." He stared into it, so I spoke softly. "I'm going back to the crowded room now. I wanted to give you a chance to sit by yourself."

He looked at me. "I like Ramona. Ramona draws. On the boardwalk, Ramona draws."

She and Bill looked toward Max. "I'll sketch you again this summer, Max." She looked at me and mouthed, "I'll watch him." Bill nodded.

I stood. "Come back in the other room when you want to, Max."

I had almost crossed the foyer when Morehouse came out of the great room, phone in one ear and a finger in the other one, so he could hear better. "The Budget Motel? And you got him?"

He nodded at me but didn't stop. As I neared the great room, he said, "You gotta be kidding."

Crime never stops.

In the great room, Megan's daughter Alicia stood behind the punch bowl, but had no takers at the moment. I grinned at her. "Bet you never thought you'd see this day."

She wore a close-fitting burgundy dress that looked great with her dark black hair. Hard to believe she was only sixteen.

"Mom did. And everybody else on the Harvest for All Committee."

I shrugged. "I was late to the party, I guess."

Scoobie swooped over and gave me a very intense kiss. My eyes widened in surprise, and then I leaned into him more.

Alicia giggled.

He pulled back somewhat and whispered. "I was too nervous to do that in front of everyone."

George spoke from a few feet away. "Nobody left yet, Scoob."

Alicia and I laughed. Scoobie took my hand and we began a slow circuit of the room. We had talked about being sure we had a conversation with each person who came, something more than 'thank you' when they offered congratulations.

We had spoken to about half of the guests when loud giggles came from near the punch table. Renée and her girls had a tall, white box, and were about to open it.

Andrew, behind them, raised his voice. "Folks, we have another main event."

Scoobie and I looked at each other and shrugged, but moved toward Renée. She pulled the sides of the box apart, which revealed a small, two-tiered wedding cake.

Julia and Michelle talked over each other. They were eager to explain they had saved money to buy the cake. "And we have things for the top," Julia finished.

I thought they might have a tiny bride and groom. Instead, they took a plastic bag from one of Aunt Madge's kitchen drawers. They extracted two plastic retrievers, a black cat, a skunk, and dollhouse size loaves of bread and cans of food.

Scoobie dropped my hand and rushed to the table. "This is so cool. " Eyes gleaming, he turned to me. "Your family is the best."

"Our family," Renée and I corrected him.

I leaned down to kiss each girl. "What a lovely surprise." I straightened. "Shall we cut it now?"

"It's too perfect," Scoobie said. He took his phone out of a pocket of his tux and took a couple of pictures. "Is later okay, girls?"

Renée responded. "Of course."

As if on cue, Julia and Michelle nodded, still smiling.

Scoobie spoke to them directly. "We want to talk to a few more guests. Then we'll cut it."

Michelle glanced at the rectangular cakes. "We can start with these."

After I blew them another kiss, Scoobie and I moved to Monica and Sylvia, two long-time Harvest for All volunteers. They sat together in what had been the front row during the ceremony. Scoobie squatted in front of them. "Ladies."

I didn't need to see him to know his eyes twinkled.

Sylvia, who often argues with him when he has crazy fundraising ideas, said, "I don't want any liquid string at the next fundraiser."

Monica had on her usual buttoned-up cardigan, but wore a dressy silver color with pearl buttons. "Oh, my."

Scoobie grinned. "I'm ordering a new sword. I think we need another Talk Like a Pirate Day."

Monica beamed. "I bought some pirate cookie cutters."

I laughed. Monica always wants to run the bake sale, and she gets muddled quickly. My eyes automatically went to Lance Wilson's photo, and back to Monica. "I can't wait to taste them."

Our attention was drawn to the back of the room. Sergeant Morehouse had returned, holding the hand of a boy about ten. One of his nephews, I assumed. Maybe he'd been asked to pick the child up at the motel. But why?

Then I looked again. Could this be the little boy from the diner?

The child had a confident walk and a brilliant smile as he came toward us. Of course, Scoobie knew Morehouse's nephews. It had to be one of them.

Scoobie stood from where he had been squatting to talk to Monica, and grinned at the boy. "Who do we have here?"

The smile faltered somewhat, but returned quickly. He pushed a shock of brown hair off his forehead and smiled back. "Your brother, goof ball."

CHAPTER ELEVEN

AUNT MADGE HADN'T MOVED so fast since she broke her ankle. She stood in front of the child and beamed down at him. "And we are so very, very glad you're here."

Scoobie's blank expression had morphed into the kind of smile I've seen him give patients in the x-ray department at the hospital. Polite, friendly, but not conveying any particular affection.

Could this really be Scoobie's brother?

I looked at Morehouse. He rarely looks confused, and his expression would have been funny any other time. "See, you two, Terry here had been waiting at the motel for his dad. They were, uh, here to see you, Scoobie."

Scoobie's face had lost some of its color. Sylvia and Monica stood to move away, both smiling at the boy as they did so.

Scoobie sat in one of the vacated chairs and patted the seat next to him. "Well, Terry, this is a special day, isn't it?"

Terry frowned. "The policeman said Dad got in an accident." He suddenly threw himself into Scoobie's arms and burst into tears. "Where is Dad?"

I sat next to the two as Scoobie pulled Terry onto his lap and patted him on the back. He was a compact little guy, with hair much darker than Scoobie's, and I thought I'd noted brown eyes rather than blue.

Terry, assuming Morehouse had the correct name, wore a pair of brown jeans with a blue dress shirt and a dark green tie. Someone had dressed him for an event of sorts, since a boy his age would usually have been in blue jeans. Who was he, really?

I looked at Scoobie and simply nodded. What could I say? Did Scoobie really have a brother? Could the sixty-something man at Ocean Alley Hospital be this child's father?

I glanced around the room. Harry and Megan stood with their backs to us, sort of blocking others' views while simultaneously emitting friendly smiles. Renée shooed her daughters toward the breakfast room, but Julia ignored her and came directly toward us.

Renée shrugged at me and propelled Michelle forward as Andrew appeared uncertain which way to go. Julia had reached Scoobie and touched the child on the back. "I think I'm your cousin now. Or something, anyway."

The sobbing stopped, and Terry turned his head toward Julia. "I have a cousin?"

She nodded. "At least two that I know of."

Scoobie's eyes met mine and went back to Terry. He flipped him so the child moved from Scoobie's lap to sit next to him, but he kept his arm around the boy's shoulder. "I don't think they have too many girl cooties."

Julia's eyes widened, and Aunt Madge broke in. "Julia, why don't you fix Terry a plate with a couple of sandwiches and some cake?"

She smiled at him. "Do you like ham or turkey?"

He brushed a hand over both eyes, and now seemed very self-conscious. "Turkey."

Whatever the circumstances, I would not contradict this child. I leaned toward him. "Terry, I'm Jolie. I'm Scoobie's wife, as of tonight, so I guess that makes me your sister-in-law."

Aunt Madge pulled up a folding chair so she faced the three of us. "And I am Jolie's aunt. And since Scoobie calls me Aunt Madge, that means you can, too."

Morehouse grabbed another chair and sat next to Aunt Madge. "Terry, I'd like to tell these guys how we got here tonight."

"You mean in your car?"

Scoobie seemed to relax, and he gave a tight grin toward Morehouse before looking at Terry. "Did he turn on a siren?"

Morehouse's expression showed mild irritation. "I have my personal car tonight. But I did get a call right after the wedding…"

"So we missed it?" Terry asked. "Dad said we were coming."

What the heck is going on?

Morehouse continued, "Mr. O'Brien didn't make it back to Budget Motel yesterday evening. Terry's been waiting for him."

Aunt Madge frowned. "Alone?"

Terry nodded. "I'm allowed to stay alone, but not usually overnight." He looked at Scoobie. "Dad went to Burger King to get me an apple pie. Where is Dad?"

"I saw him earlier. He's okay, but he had a car accident last night, and…"

Terry's mouth widened to an O and then trembled. "Is he in the hospital? Why didn't he tell you to call me?"

Scoobie's smile was tight. "He bumped his head, so he's still sleeping."

"You mean unconscious?"

Scoobie smiled more broadly. "Yes, but we hope he wakes up soon."

He looked at me, and his eyes weren't smiling. I got the message. Scoobie now had to hope that the man who deserted him would be well enough to comfort this boy.

Julia had returned with a small plate. The lopsided turkey sandwich seemed to make Terry smile as he took it. "I'm hungry."

She tried to hand the plate, now with only a piece of red velvet cake, to Scoobie. "You can hold this."

"Your arms broken?"

Julia rolled her eyes and looked at Terry as she pushed the plate toward Scoobie. "He's a pretty big dork."

Terry glanced at Scoobie, who winked at him. Seeming to agree with Julia, Terry nodded as he chewed. He seemed more at ease.

Morehouse tried again. "Terry called the station an hour or so ago. He mentioned Scoobie and the wedding. So they called me."

Aunt Madge and I said, "Thank you," and Scoobie nodded.

I turned toward where Megan and Harry had been, and realized all the guests had left the room. Harry was collecting a couple of purses, probably to take them back to guests. The reception had apparently ended. Our friends could tell we had something important to attend to.

Terry looked at Morehouse. "Should we go get my stuff?"

Morehouse smiled. "I can have another police officer do that for you." He looked at Madge.

She smiled at him and then Terry. "Would you like to sleep in the room Scoobie used for a while?"

Terry seemed puzzled. "Won't we go to Scoobie's house?"

"That depends," Scoobie said. "What do you think of pet skunks?"

Terry's eyes widened, and he had the common sense to look at Aunt Madge. "Honest?"

"Yes, but it's had its scent glands removed."

"And it usually stays under a bed," I added.

Aunt Madge gestured in a semi-circle. "We have a lot of room. We can all stay here tonight. It's a special occasion."

Terry took the cake from Scoobie. "And see Dad tomorrow?"

"Probably," Aunt Madge said. "We need to be sure he's up for visitors."

Terry had a fork halfway to his mouth, but stopped its progress. "I'm not a visitor."

"Of course you aren't. I meant we need to be sure he's awake."

The cake continued its progress to Terry's mouth, and Scoobie and I looked at each other. Our plans to stay in Ocean's Alley's Beachcomber's Alley Hotel were not important. We'd have to make a lot of impromptu decisions tonight.

Did Scoobie really have a brother, or had someone fed this kid a pile of lies?

The swinging door between the great room and breakfast room opened, and George entered. I realized he'd been gone for at least a few minutes. His almost clenched jaw implied all of the evening's earlier humor had vanished.

He came toward us and stood behind Aunt Madge's chair. "This must be Terry."

He smiled. "How did you know my name?"

George returned a smile. "A nurse at the hospital is a friend. They didn't know you were in town with your dad, since he couldn't tell them. They figured it out."

That didn't make sense to me. Why hadn't someone called Scoobie? Why call George? And why did George look so grim?

"Is my Dad okay?"

"They've been taking good care of him."

Whatever I think of George's humor or occasional barbs, he uses precise language. This response could mean the hospital had been and would continue to take care of Terence O'Brien. Or it could mean he died. Technically that would be 'they were taking care of him,' but George wouldn't say that.

Scoobie held my gaze. I saw confusion, pain, and surely anger. If they did share a father, the man had taken much better care of Terry than Scoobie. Heck, he had left Scoobie with his drunken, mean mother.

Rather than share any thoughts like that, Scoobie said, "I think when Terry is done we can give him a tour of the B&B, and introduce him to Mister Rogers and Miss Piggy."

Aunt Madge shifted in her chair. "Of course, you can lead a tour, but I know all the stories about the B&B." She looked at Terry. "May my husband Harry and I show you our home?"

Terry looked at Scoobie, with a question in his eyes.

Scoobie smiled. "She would give a better tour. And they are her dogs. It'll give me time to change out of this penguin suit, and Jolie and I can get your room ready."

Morehouse had glanced at messages on his phone, but otherwise had been unusually quiet. "Terry, my colleague, Dana, packed your stuff. We figured you wouldn't go back to the Budget Motel tonight. Food's better here."

Terry grinned. "I had everything in my bag. I was ready," he beamed at Scoobie, "to meet my brother."

Scoobie raised his palm. Terry sat his empty plate on the floor, and the two high-fived it.

Aunt Madge stood, and Harry joined her and kissed her cheek. Aunt Madge blushed. "Okay, young man. It's late."

Terry stood and addressed Harry. "So, are you my uncle now?"

The ever-genial Harry nodded. "You're going to need a scorecard, young man."

CHAPTER TWELVE

AUNT MADGE AND HARRY made a big deal about taking Terry, trailed by Julia, up the main staircase rather than the back stairs that led up from the great room. He yawned broadly as they went through the swinging door to the breakfast room, en route to the front staircase.

For several seconds, George, Scoobie, Morehouse, and I stared at each other.

George spoke first, almost in a whisper. "Listen man, I'm sorry, but your old man died about an hour ago."

Scoobie walked to the sliding glass doors and looked out on the patio for a moment. When he turned back to face us, his shoulder bumped one of the pine wreaths on the wall, which now sported a huge purple bow. It slipped to the floor, dead needles and all.

Scoobie glanced at it and shrugged. "He means nothing to me, but God, this little kid...He must have been really good to him."

I spoke slowly. "Your father knew you were getting married. He seems to have planned to...come."

Morehouse rubbed a hand over his crewcut. "So why the hell not call you?"

I headed for the loveseat, which had been pushed against the wall, and sat. Scoobie parked himself next to me. He put an arm around my shoulder and I leaned on his.

George moved a chair to face us. "Everybody knew you guys were getting married. One of the nurses texted me to call her. I, uh, thought I should go over there for a minute."

Morehouse had continued to stand as he looked at a text, but he also pulled a chair around to face us.

Scoobie shook his head. "I have got to think straight." Then he laughed, though it held no humor. "The bastard never took care of me, but I'll bet they want me to bury him."

"And because of Terry..." I stopped.

"I'll, uh, help," George said.

"Can't imagine anyone in this town would make you do it," Morehouse added.

Barking and giggles came from the floor above us. Aunt Madge had put Mister Rogers and Miss Piggy in her sewing room so they would stop trolling for tidbits. Could that have been only an hour ago? Now it seemed she had let the dogs out to roam again.

Scoobie looked upward and back at me. "Whether what he says is true or not, Terry believes every bit of it."

I added, "And no mention of a mother."

The swinging door opened, and Ramona appeared. "I don't want to butt in…"

I gestured that she should.

She entered carrying a small duffel bag. "Dana dropped off his clothes." She looked at Scoobie. "She said she took your, um, father's things to the station and she'll lock them in Morehouse's office until tomorrow."

"Thanks," Morehouse said. He looked at Scoobie. "I've sent someone back to the motel to see what kind of information your old man gave them when he registered."

Scoobie nodded and shut his eyes for a few seconds.

"Where's Renée?" I asked.

"She's putting the girls to bed," Ramona said. "She said to tell you Andrew would stay up there with them and she'll be down when they're asleep."

Scoobie pointed at one of the white guest chairs, and Ramona sat next to George.

I remembered something that surprised me at the wedding. "Ramona, where's Lester?" Ramona's uncle is only about ten years older than we are. He is almost a caricature of a low-level Jersey mob guy. Except he is a pushy real estate agent.

"He said he was getting a bad cold and didn't want to spread it."

Scoobie and George met each other's eyes, and George grinned. "So Scoob," George began. "I can handle some of the business stuff for you, but eventually you'll probably have to sign some papers."

"Thanks."

I sat up straighter. "Max. What happened to him?"

"What about him?" Scoobie asked.

"Mr. Markle took him home," George said.

I thought back to the diner. "Max said when your father talked to him for a minute at Newhart's, he had on a Veterans of Foreign Wars hat. I don't want to sound mercenary. But Uncle Gordon, he was entitled to burial in the Beverly National Cemetery."

Scoobie ran fingers through his hair. "Without the kid, I'd tell the hospital to do what they'd do to any indigent person."

Morehouse began texting again. "Could be some military records."

"Should we tell him tonight?" I asked.

Ramona shook her head, then flushed. "He'll never sleep."

Scoobie looked at me. "I guess the issue is, do we start off our relationship with this kid with a lie of omission?"

Our relationship with this kid.

"We could tell him we found out after he went to sleep…" I began.

Scoobie shook his head. "And when he's sixteen or so and asks to see the death certificate, he'll know we lied."

"Okay," I said. "We'll tell him together."

TERRY'S SOBS WOULD NOT leave my brain. Even more rooted there was his question, "What will happen to me now?"

As usual, Aunt Madge had the best response. "You'll stay with your family, of course. You have nothing to worry about."

Scoobie and I had said similar things, but Aunt Madge's instructions or guidance always seem to have a rule-of-law impact. Though I thought it right that we all accepted what Terry said – as if we'd tell an apparently orphaned child we didn't think he was one of us – I wondered why she appeared so certain.

Scoobie and I took turns sitting by his bed as Terry slept, which he finally did about two-thirty. George offered, as did Aunt Madge and Harry, but we thought Terry should see one of us if he woke up.

I leaned back in the small recliner that George and Scoobie had wrestled into the bedroom. I had taken first shift. I wanted Scoobie to have time alone if he wanted it. He did.

Terry rolled to one side, and I had a better view of his swollen eyelids. Poor little guy.

We had so many questions. Where had Terry and the so-called TAT O'Brien lived? Who told Scoobie's father we were getting married? Why did the man plan to show up here? And the ultimate question, did Terry have a mother who could care for him? Or would at least look for him?

Were Scoobie and I about to assume roles as parents? True, we expected to do so in six months or so, but a ten-year-old?

Scoobie handled kids with good humor and aplomb. He'd worked less than a year at Ocean Alley Hospital, but the Radiology Department lined up all pediatric patients with him when Scoobie was on shift. And since he worked Monday through Friday on the day shift, he had all the scheduled appointments.

I reminded myself I babysat for Michelle and Julia when I lived in Lakewood. Not a lot, but some.

When my eyes opened again, the LED light on the alarm clock said almost five A.M. Feeling panicked at being out of it for so long, I looked quickly at Terry. He still slept on his side.

I had to put my hand over my mouth not to laugh. Jazz sat on the foot of the bed, her tail curled around her, head alert. Her green eyes seemed to say that she stood guard when I didn't. She yawned and lay down to sleep.

We had left the door to the hall ajar, and it slowly opened. Scoobie stuck his head in. When he saw I was awake, he pointed at the antique rocking chair on the other side of the room. He went toward it, lifted it, and brought the rocker to sit next to me.

"You're cute when you tiptoe," I whispered.

He kept his voice equally low. "I actually slept almost three hours."

"Good!" We both looked at Terry.

Scoobie started. "How did the cat get in here?"

"No one could find her, not even Julia. You know how she is. Jazz hid until she could come out and go where she wanted."

Scoobie grunted and tilted his head toward Terry. "Are you sure you're up for this?"

Without thinking of it, I placed a hand on my now-round stomach. "I think we need to find out if there is a mother looking for him, but it doesn't sound like it."

Scoobie nodded. "Megan had an idea."

We both smiled, and I said, "Of course she did."

"She does family history research. Alicia had some school project about tracing ancestors, and Megan got hooked."

"Huh." I glanced at Terry as he stirred slightly. "Never knew that."

"Anyway, she said if we know…Terence's birthday we can put that into some online program, and we might get some information on where he's lived, maybe even marriage info. Depends on the state."

I nodded, thinking. "Ancestry, it's called. You could also do cheek swabs, you and Terry, and find out exactly how you're related."

Scoobie shrugged. "By name?"

"Don't know. I think you can find out if you have the same father."

"Something to think about. I don't want him to know I doubt him. Certainly not now."

"Agreed."

Scoobie pointed to the door. "Why don't you lie down in the next room? Even a couple hours'll help."

I covered my mouth to silence a giggle. "We slept in different beds on our wedding night."

CHAPTER THIRTEEN

BACON SMELLS WAFTED UPSTAIRS when I opened my eyes at eight A.M. How many times had I awakened in this house to smells from Aunt Madge's kitchen? I sniffed again. Muffins and cinnamon rolls, too.

A note was pinned to my sheet. I took out the straight pin and raised the paper to my eyes. "Terry and I woke up about seven. We took the dogs for a walk."

I yawned and sat up. My cream-colored wedding dress lay across a chair, and someone had put one of Aunt Madge's robes on top of it. Good, because I hadn't expected to stay at the B&B last night and had no clean clothes. A suitcase in my car would remedy that eventually.

I'll have to stuff the wedding night lingerie on the bottom for now.

Movement and voices came from down the hall. "We have to say goodbye to Terry." Julia was her usual sure-of-her-opinion self.

"And I never even really *met* him," Michelle added.

I pulled on the robe and stuck my head into the hall. A suitcase sat outside the room the girls had slept in. Apparently Andrew and Renée wanted to get on the road.

Michelle saw me and pointed. Renée turned. "Jolie. Hey." She came to me and hugged. "You okay?"

"I am. Scoobie left me a note. He and Terry are walking the dogs."

Julia had her hands on her hips. "We need to say goodbye to Terry."

Renée shrugged. "Andrew and I weren't sure if you wanted time to yourselves."

I grinned. "I'm not sure we'll have that for a while." I looked beyond her to the girls. "It's up to your mom and dad, but it's fine with me if you stay for breakfast."

"We had that, lazy bones," Michelle said.

I laughed. It felt good. "Let me go potty and I'll head down to the kitchen with you." I headed back into the bedroom Scoobie and I used and did an abbreviated set of morning ablutions in the adjoining bath. When I finished, the hallway was empty. I went down the back stairs into Aunt Madge and Harry's great room.

The room's furniture had been moved to pre-wedding placement. Aunt Madge, used to getting up at five, had been busy. I cursed myself for letting her do so much until I saw a bleary-eyed George at the oak table in the kitchen area. She had surely put him to work.

He saw me, half-smiled, and used his head to gesture toward Aunt Madge and Harry's bedroom, behind the kitchen area. "If the president needs an Army commander, she's available."

Andrew had had his back to me. Usually he has little to say to anyone, but today he turned and looked downright friendly. "Heard you guys took turns sleeping in a chair. Get used to it."

I headed toward the decaf coffee pot on a countertop. I needed hi-test, but that continued to be a no-no. "I suppose so."

The side door to the parking lot banged and Andrew nodded in that direction. "The girls dragged Renée out to look for Scoobie and…his brother, right?"

I half nodded, half shrugged. "Seems so. And Terry is quite certain."

"A lot to work through," Andrew said. "If he gets along with the girls, he can visit us."

I struggled not to tear up. Andrew offered to help someone beyond his wife and girls. "Thanks. It sounded as if the girls were ready to adopt him."

George turned toward the sound of galloping kids and barking dogs. "Dogs may be, too."

Aunt Madge and Harry had been in their bedroom suite, and came out, fully dressed and looking moderately rested. "Morning Jolie." She approached me for a kiss on the cheek as the swinging door opened.

Mister Rogers galloped into the room and skidded to a halt on the hardwood floor. Miss Piggy ran into his rump.

Aunt Madge squinted at her two fur children. "Good dogs. No running."

I wondered if I'd be able to train children as well as Aunt Madge trained her dogs. Maybe with treats.

Scoobie and Terry entered, followed by red-cheeked Michelle and Julia.

For a second Terry looked uncertain, but Julia grabbed his hand. "I want a cinnamon roll."

I blew a kiss toward Terry, and he grinned. "With frosting?"

"Sure." I took three paper plates from the stack on the counter and placed a roll on each one.

Renée came into the kitchen. "Just one."

Michelle wrinkled her nose in my direction, and Julia grabbed her plate and turned toward the breakfast room. "We'll eat in there."

Scoobie's eyes said tired, but his voice was jaunty. "I'll bring juice. Napkins are in the breakfast room."

Mister Rogers and Miss Piggy looked toward the rolls, tails wagging. I opened an upper cabinet. "Half of a biscuit."

They followed me to the sliding glass door and bolted outside. I broke the dog biscuit and threw a half at each of them. "Wow. It's cold." I shut the sliding door but stood for a moment watching them run through the snow toward where I had pitched the treats. It wouldn't take them long to sniff them out.

Renée helped herself to coffee. We joined Harry, George, Aunt Madge, and Andrew at the table as Scoobie rummaged in the fridge for a bottle of water.

George glanced toward the breakfast room as he addressed Scoobie. "Hospital said if you tell them I can make arrangements for you, all you have to do is come by and sign a couple of papers."

Scoobie downed half the bottle of water, and spoke quietly. "I need to call the funeral home, I guess."

"I did," Harry said. "Bill Oliver beat me to it."

Scoobie's tone sharpened. "What do you mean?"

Harry hesitated. "Your father's expenses will be Bill's responsibility."

Scoobie reddened.

George pointed at me. "She did solve his brother's murder. And he has a lot of money."

"How do you know?" I asked.

George shrugged. "You guys can fight with him, but he now owns the dental practice he works in up in Newark."

Scoobie regained his usual color. "I might consider it."

I sipped coffee. "Whatever you decide is fine with me."

"You should get that on tape," George said.

Giggles and voices came from the breakfast room. "Juice. Juice. Juice."

"Oh, right." Scoobie poured three glasses of orange juice from a pitcher on the counter, and encircled his hands around them as he headed toward the breakfast room.

In the silence, I looked at Renée and Andrew. "We may never know how much your daughters helped that little boy."

They both nodded, and Renée said, "I don't usually say this, but I feel as if God had a hand in them being here for him."

I smiled. "You sound like Aunt Madge."

The kids giggled as Scoobie passed out the orange juice, but I couldn't hear what he said. The whoosh of the door to the parking lot announced a new arrival.

I glanced around our group. Ramona, maybe.

Scoobie's voice rose in greeting. "Daphne! My favorite morning-after guest."

She laughed. "Watch it, Scoobie."

They talked to the kids, but I didn't hear what they said.

Aunt Madge looked at me and spoke so only those at the table could hear. "She has keys to the library, of course. I asked her to look up some photos for me."

Harry looked puzzled. "On New Year's Day?"

"I knew she wouldn't mind."

Daphne breezed in just before Scoobie. I can never tell how cold a black person is unless their teeth chatter. No red cheeks. "Hello Daphne. Missed us?"

She unwound her scarf and pointed to the coffee pot. "Not as much as that dark stuff on the counter."

Scoobie returned to the great room and planted a kiss on her cheek. "I like this dark stuff."

She laughed and swatted his shoulder. "You never change."

Scoobie bent to kiss me, and sat.

"How is Terry?" I asked.

"I'm learning bits and pieces. He did say his father, 'our dad' as he calls him, told him everything would be fine when they got to Ocean Alley. A couple things made me think Terence-cum-TAT knew he was ill."

George frowned. "You don't want to ask about it? Or his mom?"

"I'm kind of feeling my way, but I get the impression Terry thinks we had been in touch, that I knew they were coming."

Daphne placed her mug of coffee on the table, sat, and reached into her pocket. She pulled out a small envelope and passed it to Aunt Madge. "You were right. As usual."

Aunt Madge opened the unsealed envelope, pulled out a photo, and smiled. She passed it to Scoobie. "Look familiar?"

He took it and stared, his face expressionless. Then he lifted his eyes to mine and handed the photo to me.

A newspaper clipping showed a pumpkin carving at Ocean Alley Elementary, more than twenty years ago. The children poking fingers through the pumpkin's vacant eyes were not identified by name, but anyone who knew him would recognize an approximately eight-year-old Scoobie.

Harry looked at the photo-sized article as I held it. "How on earth did you remember that one picture?"

"I took it." Aunt Madge nodded at Scoobie. "Your teacher, Miss Anderson, was my friend. I made the cake for the party that day."

Scoobie stared at her.

"Miss Anderson donated her class scrapbooks to the library when she died. The glue had dried, so I went through them to paste some of the photos and things back in."

I passed the photo to George, but looked at Scoobie. He had no photos of himself until about high school, pictures friends had taken at various times. I'd never seen a picture of him this young. "He does look a lot like you."

Scoobie blew out a breath. "He does."

"Darker hair," George said.

"Yes." Aunt Madge reclaimed the photo from George. "One of the few differences, though." She looked at it again and spoke softly. "Terry's been better cared for."

Scoobie clenched and unclenched his jaw. "Seems so."

None of us had been aware of the sounds from the breakfast room, so we jumped as three kids barreled into the great room.

"That's really good frosting!" Michelle said.

"Oh good," Andrew murmured. "A sugar high."

Aunt Madge tilted her head toward a counter at the far end of her kitchen. "I hope you don't mind another one. We need to cut that cake."

Julia and Michelle said, "Yes," and fist-bumped each other.

Terry looked toward it. "I don't even remember that from last night."

Aunt Madge lifted the cake and placed it on her oak table. "Clear off mugs and plates, folks." She went to a drawer and took out a knife with a white handle. "Let's get a few pictures." She looked at me. "Scamper upstairs you two, put on your wedding finery."

I glanced at my bathrobe. "You're right. This won't do. We won't be long."

By the time Scoobie and I came back down, the few dishes were done and someone had placed the nosegay Michelle and Julia gave me in front of the cake. Scoobie and I had combed our hair and I'd put on lipstick, but basically, it would be a come-as-you-are kind of photo.

Harry had his camera, and he lined up first the Gentil family, then family plus anyone else in the room. Then he set the camera's timer and joined the photo himself.

Through all the picture taking, I thought Terry's smiles were forced. Who could blame him? He'd only know us a few hours.

Aunt Madge clapped her hands briskly. "I have a suggestion." She smiled at Terry. "Since Scoobie has just met his brother, I think Terry should help Jolie and Scoobie cut the cake."

His look of surprise turned to delight. "I can help with that."

Harry took several pictures. I demurred on feeding one another cake. Scoobie started to playfully insist, but when I patted my baby bump, he got it. Dry toast usually avoided morning sickness, cake was a no-no.

Andrew stood and gestured to the kids. "Come on upstairs you three. Terry can help you girls finish packing."

At Terry's fading smile, Andrew added, "If timing works out, they can visit for a bit on Sunday."

As they tromped up the back stairs I turned to Renée. "That would be good for him to look forward to. It's okay?"

"Sure." She looked at Scoobie. "If you do a funeral or something I'll try to bring them down. I don't think there are any big tests at school next week."

Scoobie nodded to her but looked at me. "Now that you've seen Terry more, you really think he was in the diner with TAT?"

"What?" Harry asked.

"It means The Absent Terence," Scoobie said.

"I meant the diner bit is new to me."

Aunt Madge squirmed a bit. "Jolie thought she may have seen Terence talking to Elmira. And maybe Max.

Arnie is going to go through his security company to check it out."

Harry frowned. "I hadn't heard that."

I spoke quickly. "Thanks to me and wedding plans, you've been working too much. Sorry I forgot to tell you."

Harry's "Humph" said he knew he'd been kept in the dark on purpose. Not by me. Maybe Aunt Madge didn't want him to think she kind of snooped. It's gotten her in trouble before.

CHAPTER FOURTEEN

ON NEW YEAR'S DAY, Ocean Alley's streets were quiet. No doubt retail sales meant the mall outside of town bustled, but people not shopping were hunkered down at home. I yawned.

En route to the funeral home, Terry and Scoobie shared the front seat. Aunt Madge had spoken to Funeral Director Martin Peters. We thought that he – as a father of four and grandfather of seven – could have a casual conversation with Terry. Peters would ask some of the questions Terry believed Scoobie and I already knew the answers to.

We were grateful for any suggestions. We didn't want to live a lie. It simply seemed that Terry had had enough blows. Telling him we had never heard of him seemed almost cruel.

Scoobie explained to Terry that we were going to the funeral home "for a visit." He stressed that they would not be seeing "our dad" yet. I knew it killed him to say those words.

I didn't really know Martin Peters other than saying hello at a couple of viewings. Aunt Madge knew him largely because he'd been one of the few men on the Ocean Alley Hospital Auxiliary. I pushed aside an unkind thought that perhaps he saw the volunteer work as a way to meet sick people.

Terry said little as we drove, but he responded politely when I spoke. "Terry, you see that store? That's where Scoobie's and my friend Ramona works."

He craned his neck to look at The Purple Cow. "They don't have cows at the beach."

"It's an office supply store. School supplies, too."

That seemed to interest him. "Dad had me turn in my books at my old school." He turned to Scoobie. "Will you take me to my new school?"

"Yep. I need to find out which one. We have two elementary schools."

"I'm in *middle* school."

Scoobie gave him a quick grin and put his eyes on the road again. "Sorry. We only have one of those."

"It's okay." He sighed. "Everyone says I'm short."

"I'm not too tall, and I didn't get much of a growth spurt until high school. You'll grow."

Terry sat up straighter.

We pulled into the funeral home parking lot. Like Aunt Madge's house, Peters Funeral Home had been a single-family Victorian home that now had another purpose. Much bigger than the Cozy Corner, it had a one-story addition in the back that I assumed was where they did embalming. Not that I wanted to think about that now.

Terry stopped when we got to the bottom of the steps that led to the porch.

Scoobie put an arm around his shoulder. "You don't have to go in, buddy."

He sighed. "I knew this would happen someday. I mean," he looked at Scoobie. "Dad was kinda old. Compared to my friends' dads."

Scoobie frowned lightly. "Age isn't the most important thing."

Terry started up the steps. "So, if you're thirty-one, is that the same age Dad was when you were born?"

Scoobie paused, but then resumed the climb up the steps next to Terry. "About the same."

As we stepped onto the wide porch, the front door opened and Martin Peters smiled at us. "A good day for hot chocolate, I think."

I relaxed somewhat. It seemed he'd thought about how to help Terry feel more at ease.

Peters looked into a room just off the funeral home foyer. "Maria. How about four hot chocolates?"

"Sure thing." She walked toward the back of the building. I didn't know Maria, who looked about seventy. Her mid-calf black dress and the crucifix she wore around her neck made me think Italian, like a lot of people in Ocean Alley.

Mr. Peters led us down a wallpapered hallway through a doorway on the right. Thick carpet and a Chippendale-style table with a high sheen lent the room a sense of understated formality.

Scoobie stood against the wall, but where we could make eye contact, and I sat in one of the two chairs opposite Peters' desk. I patted the chair next to me and Terry sat. For the first time, he looked truly anxious. I wanted to hug him, but maybe he wouldn't like it. *How do I help a grieving kid?*

Mr. Peters sat and smiled at Terry. "You look about the same age as my grandson. He's eleven."

Terry brightened. "Does he go to middle school here?"

"In fact, he does. I can introduce you if you like."

Scoobie spoke. "When do the kids go back to school?"

"Since the second is a Friday, not until the fifth." He returned his gaze to Terry. "I'm sorry about your dad. I know it's tough."

Terry blinked a few times. "Thank you. Now what do we do?"

Peters' nod was solemn. "Scoobie and Jolie, and I guess Madge, will plan a memorial service with you. They can do all of it, if you..."

"I want to."

Peters smiled. "I thought you would. In fact, you can help me with a couple of things."

More blinking, and Terry asked, "Like what?"

Peters tapped a manila folder on his desk. "You folks can look at some of these sample prayers and hymns, but first I wanted to ask you about how we can let people where you used to live know that your dad has passed."

"In Panama City, you mean?"

Scoobie and I exchanged a brief glance. *Bingo.*

"Yes." He never took his gaze off Terry. "I can place a notice in the local paper, of course, but are there any special friends I should contact? A church, perhaps?"

Terry frowned. "Dad said my new school would contact my old one. I guess you should tell them at the base, but I'm not sure..."

Scoobie and I stayed quiet. These were things it seemed Terry expected us to know. Maybe someday we'd tell him Terence O'Brien had not talked to his oldest son in close to twenty years, but not now.

"Did you guys live on base?"

Terry smiled. "Course not. Our apartment was near the beach, not at Tyndall."

Peters continued eye contact with him. "Of course. I guess you guys went to the PX, huh?"

He shrugged. "Not so much. But my dad went to meetings with some people from the base." He frowned. "I met some, but I don't know phone numbers or anything."

Scoobie cleared his throat and Terry looked at him. "If you even know first names, I bet I can find people."

Terry tilted his head. "I dunno."

Scoobie smiled. "Anonymous meetings, maybe?"

Terry grinned broadly. "Yep."

Scoobie nodded. "I go to those sometimes, mostly with George. We can figure it out."

Terry looked at me. "Do you go?"

"Not as often, but some."

Scoobie cleared his throat. "If you know where he went to his meetings, maybe we can drive down there sometime and you can let his friends know you're okay."

Terry shrugged. "I think they know. I mean, they don't know dad died." He frowned. "But they know we were coming here. You know, because of the cancer."

Scoobie's expression didn't change, but he stiffened. "It's a good thing you got here."

"It sure is." Terry squirmed in his chair, and he looked at the floor rather than Scoobie. "And you're sure it's okay? Dad said he didn't know how big your house is."

I tapped Terry's shoulder. "It may not be large, but we have room. Plus, our friend Lester has been trying to sell us a bigger house."

Terry brightened. "You think I can have my own room?"

I saw Scoobie's humor kick into gear before he spoke. "You don't mind sharing with the skunk do you?"

Terry looked dubious as he turned to more directly face Scoobie. "Aunt Madge said it didn't stink, right?"

Peters cleared his throat. "So, Terry, I have a couple more questions."

Terry faced him. "Okay."

"I'm sorry if these questions are hard for you, but I wonder if you'd like me to mention your father's illness in his obituary?"

Terry frowned. "He went to the doctor before the cancer, but I don't know everything."

Thankfully, Terry focused intently on Peters. He didn't see Scoobie lean against the wall. Did some long-term illness explain why his father had left, why he never contacted Scoobie?

Maybe, but it didn't explain how The Absent Terence O'Brien had managed to raise such a confident, loving second child. Heck, it could be his fifth child for all we knew.

Peters nodded at Terry. "I'm only asking because sometimes people like to mention a family member's illness. It's not essential."

Terry's bottom lip trembled. "I don't know all of it."

I put a hand on Terry's shoulder, and Scoobie moved to kneel in front of him. "It's not up to you to know."

Peters rose and took a folding chair from a small closet behind his desk. He carried it to Scoobie, who opened it and sat.

Terry sniffed and wiped one finger under his nose. "You don't know either?"

Peters reached for a tissue, but didn't proffer it yet.

Scoobie shook his head. "No, we sure didn't. I know he would have liked to talk about...some things."

Some things? Like why he left Scoobie but raised this child and then brought him to us when he seemed to know he was dying?

Before anyone spoke again, a light rap came from the door.

Peters grinned at Terry. "Hot chocolate. Come in!"

Maria backed into the office with a tray, and Scoobie jumped up to hold the door. "Can't have you spilling the good stuff."

Terry leaned back in his chair, seeming more relaxed. "Don't drink it too fast, or you'll burn your tongue."

"Good advice," I said. As Maria placed the tray on Peters' desk, I stood to hand a mug to Terry. I leaned it toward the window. "Not too much steam. Test it, though."

He accepted the mug with both hands, sniffed the drink, and took a small sip. Cream on top gave him a white mustache, and his smile was infectious. "I think I'm going to like this place."

Mr. Peters guided the rest of the conversation to the Ocean Alley Middle School mascot, an orange sea horse, and youth soccer leagues. "Tryouts for the spring teams are sometime in February, but pretty much anyone can play."

Terry listened intently. "We played soccer during recess. I mean, in grade school. We don't have recess in middle school."

"What are your favorite subjects?" I asked.

"First is math."

Scoobie pointed a finger at me. "Don't ask Jolie for help."

I stuck my tongue out rather than show him my finger. "Algebra's fine. Don't ask about geometry. Any chance you like to write stories?"

"Like Dad, you mean?" He grinned at Scoobie.

Another gut punch for Scoobie. "Or your own kind?"

Scoobie's expression did not change. I thought my husband would qualify for an Academy Award.

Terry seemed to want Scoobie to say something. "Did you look in my bag? I have your old book."

Scoobie cleared his throat. "I bet you have more than one of my old books."

"Nope. Just the blue one. With the color pictures."

Scoobie nodded slowly. "*A Child's Garden of Verses*."

"Yep. Dad read it to me some. On the drive here, he said you asked him to read it to you every night." He frowned. "But, um, I didn't mean to get chocolate milk on it."

Scoobie took a tissue from the box on Peters' desk and blew his nose. "A little milk never hurt anything."

I thought this might be getting too close to Scoobie's more raw emotions, so I looked at Peters.

He took the hint. "We have a wonderful library here. In fact," he looked at Scoobie, "I used to see you in there a lot."

Scoobie seemed surprised that Peters would have noticed, but nodded.

Peters smiled at Terry. "Your brother writes poems, you know."

"Wow."

Scoobie had regained his jaunty attitude, at least on the surface. "You can tell me what you think after you read a few."

I tried to maintain the cheerful tone. "They're good. Maybe not all the ones about pirates."

Peters had finished his hot chocolate, and his attitude became more businesslike. I figured he had another appointment.

"So, Terry, why don't you take this folder of hymns and prayers with you? You can talk about them with Scoobie and Jolie."

"Even better," I added, "Aunt Madge and Harry. Aunt Madge knows a lot more prayers than I do."

Terry yawned broadly, but stopped abruptly. "What church do we use? For Dad's funeral?"

I nodded at Scoobie. "Aunt Madge and Harry are members of a great church, First Presbyterian."

"First Prez," Scoobie said.

"Don't you go?" Terry asked.

"We were just there on Christmas," I said. "We don't go every Sunday, but Aunt Madge does."

Peters saw a practical opening. "Did you and your dad go to a particular church in Florida?"

Terry reached to the desk and took the folder. "Me and Mom went to St. Augustine's. Sometimes after she died, Dad and I went to the chapel on the base, but not a lot." He yawned again.

I looked at Peters. "We were all up late."

"You can say that again." Terry frowned toward Peters. "So, do we use Aunt Madge's church?"

Peters nodded. "You can. You can also have a service in the chapel here. Sometimes people do that when they don't know a lot of people in the area."

Terry looked dubious.

Peters stood. "Scoobie and Jolie know what our chapel looks like. How about if they follow us while I show you?"

We trailed behind, and I heard Peters explain that families could use a small sitting room they passed."

I took Scoobie's hand, and spoke softly. "I suppose we have a couple of starting points."

Scoobie squeezed my fingers. "I guess so. Hard to know how we'll learn a lot more."

I figured we could come up with facts — the name of Terry's school, maybe a medical clinic that treated TAT. Basically, we knew more about Terry and his father, but not much more about how Terence O'Brien had evolved from deserter to attentive parent. Scoobie needed to know that.

CHAPTER FIFTEEN

TERRY WANTED TO SHOW Scoobie what he called the blue book, so they went upstairs while I sat with Aunt Madge and Harry in their kitchen.

Aunt Madge studied me. "You look drained."

"I'm only tired. Probably should have a short baby nap." When they both regarded me, I added, "I really like that little boy. It's just...a lot."

Mister Rogers' bark came from the floor above us, and Terry's voice drifted down the stairs. "And they definitely don't bite, right?"

Aunt Madge glanced at the ceiling and then smiled at me. "He is a sweetheart."

"What did you learn?" Harry asked.

"They lived in Panama City, Florida, and Terry's dad had some kind of affiliation with Tyndall Air Force Base. Oh, and he's in middle school, not elementary."

Harry got up and walked toward their bedroom. "Be right back."

"Probably getting his computer," Aunt Madge said.

When Harry moved in, she'd agreed to get Internet service in the B&B. Prior to that, she maintained people came to the beach for relaxation, and would not add it. I always thought she didn't want to fool with modems and such.

I nodded. "I bet he can find something."

"How was Mr. Peters with him?"

"Terrific. Asked just a few questions, had hot chocolate for us. Oh, and he gave Terry a folder with some prayers and hymns. We thought you might be better to discuss some of it with Terry."

"As long as you participate. Any thoughts about a service?"

"Peters showed him the chapel at the funeral home. You think that would be good?"

She tilted her head slightly upward. "Anything is fine, but smaller scale might be easier for both of them."

Harry returned and plopped his laptop on the table. "What was his full name?"

"Terence Adam O'Brien."

That reminded me of an earlier question and I pointed a finger at Aunt Madge. "You knew that. And Scoobie thought you'd know what his father looked like."

"I didn't know the man well, but Uncle Gordon knew him."

"Uncle Gordon! A friend of his?"

She shook her head. "More an acquaintance from a veterans' group. Scoobie's father was a lot younger than Gordon. I doubt Scoobie knew they were friends. I'm just of an age to remember what Terence O'Brien looked like."

Harry looked up from his keyboard. "So, how old would Scoobie have been when Gordon died?"

Aunt Madge nodded at me. "He and Jolie were both five at that time. Of course, they didn't know each other. Terence came to Uncle Gordon's wake."

Scoobie spoke from the base of the stairs. "No sh...kidding."

I patted the table next to me, and he sat. "Is Terry asleep?"

"He almost dove into bed." He glanced at Aunt Madge. "It's okay that the dogs stay up there? I left the door to the bedroom half open."

The two of them locked eyes, and she asked, "Do you remember being at the funeral home for my Gordon, with your father?"

Scoobie shook his head. "I know my father stayed until I was about twelve. I remember not understanding why he left, but most of my memories are horrible things my mother said after he had gone."

Aunt Madge sighed. "He took you around town with him often, since he didn't...have a traditional job."

"My mother said he never worked. I don't...I just don't remember much about him."

Harry said, "You might want to look at this." He turned his laptop so we could see it. "I have a subscription to a public records database, for business, you know? I put Terence O'Brien's name into it. For Florida."

We looked at the listing for Terence Adam O'Brien of Panama City, Florida. He had apparently lived in two different apartments over the last eight years. Part of the record listed "others in household," and showed a woman's name. Marti O'Brien. Terence O'Brien's age range indicated 60-65, but she had no age mention.

Harry pointed to her name. "When there is no age, it can mean deceased. She's still shown as associated with him because, probably, they were married. Could have had credit cards together, and he may not have closed an account."

Scoobie put his elbows on the table and cradled his head in his hands. "I can't believe this is real."

I put a hand on his shoulder. "I'm sorry, babe."

He turned his head toward me, with a trace of a smile. "If you don't stop saying you're sorry I'll make a list of past transgressions you can apologize for."

Aunt Madge's tone was dry. "I'm sure it will be a long one."

I ignored her. "Did you see Terry's blue book?"

Scoobie lifted his head and sat back in the chair. "Yes. I treasured that book of poems. I always wondered what happened to it." His expression grew grim. "My mother threw out all my books at one point. So now I, or Terry and I, have one."

A LOT OF PEOPLE had January 2nd off for a long weekend, but most government offices were open. When Scoobie went to work Friday morning, I headed for the courthouse.

Even if it had previously occurred to me to look up information on Scoobie's father, I wouldn't have done that. Plus, I hadn't even known the man's full name.

Most of our time together Scoobie has been opposed to me snooping, as he calls it. Today he wanted me to see what I could learn about his father's years in Ocean Alley.

Skies were clear, but a cold wind almost blew me up the courthouse steps. I couldn't wait to get indoors. I shivered as I stomped my feet and glanced around the tiled lobby. Facing it were several huge oak doors that led to either courtrooms or offices.

Miller County is the smallest in New Jersey, and its courthouse is sized accordingly. The building is at least the second one, though I suppose there were earlier courthouses, given that New Jersey is one of the original states.

Built in the early 1920s, its predecessor had been severely damaged by fire. Uncle Gordon's mother served as the county elections clerk at the time. She heard the fire engines and ran to the building in her bath robe to try to save records.

When the firefighters refused to let her in, she snuck in the back and closed several of the heavy interior oak doors, which kept the fire from spreading into more offices. I bless her every time I hunt for prior sales data on properties I'm appraising.

I glanced at the transom above one of those very doors, which had been rehung in the new courthouse, and let myself into the county clerk's office. Given my many record searches, I'd grown familiar with which files were kept locally. Basically, only municipal and county records were here. I glanced at a screen that explained these were largely for lesser infractions – or accusations of them.

In the courthouse, I could search statewide indexes for other courts or types of records, but my interest was Miller County. Likely Terence O'Brien had had a few brushes with Ocean Alley police. What those would tell me, I didn't know.

Along the wall in the clerk of court's office sat two computers the public could use to search court cases and their dispositions. I'd used them previously, but not recently. I noted I could search by name, date, or type of offense. I wondered whether the electronic data would go back far enough.

I opened the search screen and smiled. Municipal Court online indexes dated from even before Scoobie's father left the family. After reading a couple of other screens, I figured out that if TAT had a traffic arrest or maybe a burglary, he'd be in Municipal Court records. More serious charges would have sent him to Superior Court, which also had a courtroom in the Miller County Courthouse.

I started with TAT's full name, reminding myself I had to get used to saying Terence instead of TAT, and said I wanted references from any year. The brevity surprised me. Two public drunkenness charges, an altercation with an officer, and a request for a restraining order (one O'Brien against the other).

No divorce information. I went back to the computer explanation screens. Superior Court handled divorce, which the New Jersey courts called dissolution. "Nuts." I needed to know the year to be able to find records.

I reviewed what I had found in the Municipal Court database. The public drunkenness charges were both on the boardwalk, and the cases were adjudicated without a trial. The fine for the second was pretty hefty.

The database had no details on the case involving the altercation. I was surprised it had gone to trial, more surprised with the resolution for 'referral for mental health treatment.' I bet Scoobie didn't know about that.

The restraining order mentioned was simply an index item. I had no way to know the circumstances.

I searched for the name of the attorney who represented Terence O'Brien. I had met Sam Jefferson because my high school classmate, and now Miller County Prosecuting Attorney Annie Milner, had invited him to a meeting I attended. Since I'd simply sat across from him as Annie got her campaign organized, I didn't really know him.

I jotted the case number and lawyer's name, then went back to the list of Terence O'Brien cases to note the case numbers for the public drunkenness charges. Sam Jefferson had been TAT's attorney for those, too. Perhaps he and the senior O'Brien were close in age. Maybe they'd been classmates at Ocean Alley High.

I glanced at my watch. I told Aunt Madge I wouldn't leave Terry with her for more than an hour. I needed to get going.

For fifty cents a page, a rip-off, I printed those relating to the public drunkenness charges, the restraining order, and the altercation that led to the mental health treatment. If Scoobie wanted to know more about his parents' marital problems, he could visit Superior Court. I didn't want him to think I pried into information that personal. Or ugly.

I folded the papers and put them in my purse as I left the clerk of court's office. Then I pulled them out and sat on one of the long benches in the courthouse lobby.

"Jolie! What are you doing here? Harry isn't making you work, is he?"

Dana Johnson is my favorite Ocean Alley police officer. We're close in age, and Scoobie and I had invited

Dana and her husband to the wedding. She had to work. While she won't break any rules, she'll sometimes talk to me about a case. Sergeant Morehouse tells me to butt out. Regularly.

"No, of course not. I'm uh…" I glanced at the closed door behind me and lowered my voice. "You know about Terry, of course."

Her frown expressed concern. "He really is Scoobie's brother?"

I shrugged. "We aren't about to do DNA tests, not now anyway. But Aunt Madge says he looks a lot like Scoobie from back then."

Dana looked dubious.

"She knew how to find a picture of Scoobie in school. Not quite twin-ish, but you see the resemblance immediately."

She studied me. "Huh."

"You here to testify on something?"

She nodded. "Traffic case. Some bozo…" she grinned. "I mean taxpaying citizen, swears our radar guns were wrong when we clocked him going 60 in the 40-mile zone out near Wal-Mart."

"I remember George got a ticket near there, when he rushed to cover a story for the paper."

She raised her eyebrows. "Did he tell you he had two prior warnings?"

I laughed loud enough that a man heading into the county treasurer's office glared at me. "Of course he didn't."

"Figures. Is Terry going to stay with you guys?"

"I suppose. " I patted my stomach. "Bit earlier than we thought we'd have a kid."

"More power to you." She pointed at a nearby door that led to the registrar's office. "What are you doing, filing your marriage certificate?"

I grinned fully. "That's the responsibility of the person who performs the service."

"Oh, good. You've seen all the crap George keeps in his car."

"I should probably have Scoobie check." I raised the papers I held. "Looking at records for Scoobie's dad. Before he left."

Her eyes narrowed. "What on earth do you expect to find?"

Until I said it, I hadn't known why I had come here first, instead of searching library databases for Florida newspapers or something like that. "The reason his father left."

"You met Scoobie's mother."

I grunted. "And you did, too. Still, for him to leave Scoobie with her seems…" I let my voice trail off.

She nodded. "I hear you. Scoobie know what you're doing?"

I tried to keep my irritation from showing. "Why do people always ask me that?"

"They know you." She pointed toward the courtroom door across the lobby. "See you later."

I sat back on the bench and leafed through the pages again. Terence O'Brien had the public drunkenness charges, but never a DUI. Or one where charges were filed, anyway.

The final page I'd copied had brief information on the request for a restraining order, which had been denied. I skimmed it, wishing I could see what Terence

O'Brien had done to make his wife request he be kept away.

I stopped mid-page. He had made the request to keep the then Penny O'Brien away from *him*. "Damn." I skimmed through the list of court actions associated with the case. He had not shown up for the hearing. A judge dismissed the request.

What was the date? Why didn't he pursue it? I couldn't tell.

O'Brien made the request two weeks after Scoobie's twelfth birthday. Right around the time he left, from what Scoobie knew.

I grew so flushed I slid out of my coat. If Terence O'Brien thought his wife was a danger to him, why the devil didn't he take his son with him?

CHAPTER SIXTEEN

I RATIONALIZED THAT MY upcoming trip to the library would give Scoobie a fuller sense of his father's life after he left Ocean Alley. I had also told him I would contact the Air Force base before Scoobie got off work at three. We weren't sure what we could learn there. Something. Anything.

I had the phone number for an organization called the 'community relations office' in my purse. I parked in the Cozy Corner parking lot and pulled out the paper. My plan had been to call from inside, with a cup of tea. It occurred to me I might not want Terry to hear every word. I'd have to get used to thinking like that.

I took a breath as I pulled my mobile phone from my purse. There couldn't be as many surprises with this call as there were at the courthouse.

An official-sounding man answered. "Tyndall Community Relations. How can I help you?"

"I'm not sure, so let me tell you who we are first." I explained that Scoobie was Terry's brother, and their father had been Terence O'Brien."

"Did you say 'had been,' ma'am?" The voice now sounded less official and more like a real person.

"Yes. I'm sorry to tell you, but he died a couple of days ago. In New Jersey."

"But Terry is with you? Is he all right? Who are you again?" Now the man sounded as if he really cared.

I spoke for almost a full minute, relaying how Terence's plan had been to introduce the two brothers himself, and that he had just missed doing that. Then I explained my role, and that Terry was being well cared for. "In fact, he's with my aunt, now also his aunt, learning how to cook."

He expelled a breath. "I'm Sergeant Francis Booker. Terry's mom, Marti, and I were in the same unit for almost a year. I'm…I'm so sorry about Terence."

Finally I knew something about Terry's mother beyond her name on the computer search Harry did yesterday. "Sounds like you and Marti and Terence were friends."

"I didn't know Terence well until after Marti passed. The Air Force helped him with death benefits and all that, but Terence also came to me a couple of times to help navigate the paperwork. As Marti's friend."

I didn't realize I'd been holding my breath until I blew it out. "They were so lucky to have you. Since we didn't have a chance to talk to Terry's dad recently, it's good to find someone who knew them in Florida."

"And…" Francis Booker paused.

"Yes?"

"Terence had planned to introduce Terry to people in the town where he grew up, but we didn't, uh, actually know that Terry had a brother. Especially an adult brother."

I had to tread carefully here. "Terence and my husband, Scoobie – actually Adam, but he doesn't use the name – planned to talk a lot more." *Well, Terence planned it. Only half a lie.*

"And..." the man paused for several seconds, "I'm sorry if this sounds so personal. We actually thought Terence and Terry were leaving after the first of the year, until we got a thank-you card New Year's Eve. Are you...do you have other children?"

Finally, a familiar topic. "We're expecting our first in roughly six months."

"That's great. Terry will have a..." he hesitated.

I laughed. "A nephew. Do you have children?"

"No, ma'am." Francis Booker's tone grew official again. "If it's okay, there are a couple of us who would probably like to stay in touch with Terry."

"I'm sure it will be..."

"Has the funeral been held? Or is there one planned? I'd like to be there for Terry."

I hesitated. The man sounded as if he cared, but I had no idea if Terry would want to see him. "We haven't fixed on a date, but it will be in the next few days. I really need to talk to my husband, and Terry, about...who to invite."

His tone grew insistent. "Tell Terry it's his mom's friend Frank. My wife and I, her name's Linda, we would both try to come. Tell him we'll bring the cookies she makes. The ones with M&Ms. He likes them a lot."

A couple thoughts fell into place. Francis' wife made cookies Terry liked. They'd been close to Marti. They may have viewed Terry as much more than the son of an older, recently widowed, man.

My eyes started to tear. "I can't believe I found someone who knows them so well."

"It is lucky. But anyone here can help you." His tone had grown more formal again. "I took you off your mission. What can I do for you today?"

I thought carefully. I didn't want to reveal how little we knew. "The funeral home could require a copy of Marti's death certificate."

"Sure. Let's see."

I could almost hear his brain whirring.

"It could take a few days to get a certified copy for you. She died in the base hospital, so I think we can get it here. I can probably get a photo copy from her file. It's relatively recent, I think the paper file is probably still on base."

I hesitated. "You sound as if you knew them really well. We, uh, don't know where Terry's mom is buried, or if she and his dad had joint plots..." I deliberately let my voice trail off.

"She was cremated, ma'am. Her remains are in the Columbarium at Tallahassee National Cemetery."

When I said nothing, he added, "That's a cemetery for military personnel and their spouses."

"I see. So, should we should arrange for, I'm not sure how to ask, transport of, uh, Terence's ashes?" My first thought was that cremation might be hard for Terry to handle, then I had a duh moment and realized he would have dealt with such issues after his mom died.

Frank Booker's pause was so long I thought we had lost the connection.

"The thing is, ma'am..."

"Jolie."

"Right. Marti is in a space that can accommodate Terence, but the thing is, the cremation idea was hard on Terry. It is for a lot of kids. Of course, it's economical, and the military maintains the Columbariums with the same respect as all graves."

"I...understand. We, well, we and friends, would be able to have a, um, more traditional burial. But it would have to be here. That would mean Terry's parents would be in two places."

"If you can do that, it might be easier for him. At some point, Marti's remains could be placed in the same plot as her husband's. At least, you can talk to the cemetery about that."

"Oh, that would be perfect. I mean, not perfect." *What a dumb thing to say!*

"You mean it would be making the best of a bad situation. It's tough to lose both your parents when you're ten."

"Thanks. That's a much better way to put it. We can talk to the funeral director in our town about that."

"Just so you know," Booker said, "Terry did not want to go to the funeral home for his mom. He did, of course, but it took a lot of coaxing."

I remembered how Terry had paused at the funeral home steps. "We took him for what we called a visit with the funeral director. He's a friend of my aunt's. Terry seemed a bit hesitant, but they had hot chocolate for him, and Scoobie was able to help him a lot."

Booker expelled a breath. "Thank God he was in your town."

I told him I'd call back with the funeral home fax number. He gave me his and his wife's cell phones and their home phone. I felt as if no lottery jackpot could ever feel like a bigger win.

After ending the call I sat in the car, decompressing, for more than a minute. I pulled the court papers about Terence – that seemed like something I'd done days ago – and jotted a note about Marti and the Bookers on the back of one of the pages. I would hand it to Aunt Madge, and tell Scoobie after I checked on Terry.

By the time I entered the B&B, my smile was in place.

When Aunt Madge offered to teach Terry to bake bread, he had been thrilled at the idea. I planned to pick him up to go to the library, and didn't see why what I learned would change that. I had told him we might meet some kids his age, or find a flyer about a soccer league or something.

I expected the kitchen would look kind of like when I tried to make a cake from scratch. Flour on the counter, sink piled with measuring cups and bowls. Hopefully no slippery egg on the floor.

Wrong. Terry stood on Aunt Madge's step stool, elbow-deep in bread kneading. Aunt Madge leaned against the neat counter, her face beaming approval. Not a look I usually saw when I tried to cook.

Terry turned his head as I came through the swinging door. He smiled broadly. "Aunt Madge says I'm really good at this."

She nodded. "A natural eye for measuring precisely, and very good at punching the rising bread. I told him he could teach you a couple of things."

I smiled at Terry, and when he turned his back, I stuck my tongue out at Aunt Madge. "I bet it will smell good in here in a few minutes."

He didn't look at me, but Terry said, "It always smells good here."

Great that he feels at home.

"It does." I held up the papers and placed them on the oak table.

Aunt Madge headed in that direction. I unzipped my jacket and crossed the kitchen to stand next to Terry. Aunt Madge had rolled his sleeves almost to his biceps, and the dough squelched as he kneaded it.

I leaned on the counter next to him. "How did you avoid getting flour everywhere?"

His eyes shifted toward me and back to his bread. "You just have to go kinda slow."

Aunt Madge tittered, but I ignored her. "I thought you and I could eat some of that bread when it comes out of the oven, and I could show you more of Ocean Alley. Maybe stop at the library."

He stopped and turned his head. "Can I get my own card?"

"I don't see why not."

My phone chirped, so I moved a few steps from Terry to look at a text message.

Scoobie's message said, "I need to talk to you, but not where anyone else can hear. Call me in 10."

Though he'd never sent such a message, given everything going on – including funeral planning – it didn't seem that odd. I texted back, "Going upstairs in a minute. Call anytime."

Aunt Madge glanced up from the court case info I'd given her and widened her eyes as if to say, "Wow." She pointed to my purse, indicating she would put the papers there when she finished with them.

I nodded. "I'm going upstairs to pack our last couple of things."

Terry looked up. "For when we go to Scoobie's house?"

I wrinkled my nose at him. "For when we go to Scoobie's, mine, and your house."

He gave a quick grin and turned back to his bread.

Aunt Madge stood to wave me upstairs. "Terry, I'll show you how to shape it to put in the pans."

I trudged up the back staircase. As I neared the room Scoobie and I had shared last night, my phone chirped again, this time a call. "Hey."

"Jolie." Scoobie sounded unusually serious. "I talked to the medical examiner a few minutes ago."

A couple doctors performed this function at the hospital, usually an older woman named Dr. O'Malley. Aunt Madge knew her, of course. "Oh?"

"They were getting the death certificate ready, and the doctor found some things she didn't like."

I had to stifle a giggle. *Damn hormones!* "So...isn't that common when someone dies?"

"Not like this. They found an unexpected drug in TAT's blood."

I absorbed Scoobie's words, but didn't understand. "So drugs could be unexpected, but what does it mean?"

"It means the seizure or heart attack when his car crashed could be because someone tried to kill him."

CHAPTER SEVENTEEN

"KILL HIM? THAT DOESN'T make any sense." I could hear the panic in my tone and tried to calm myself.

"You didn't know him."

I sat on the bed. The calm of the beautifully decorated bedroom made his words even more surreal. "Scoobie, you're right, I didn't. But think about it. Who in town expected him?"

"It might not have been someone here." Scoobie paused. "The medical examiner said that he could have been given a drug over time. Maybe it had a cumulative effect."

"Did she say what drug?"

"No. I don't think I'm supposed to know yet. I stopped by the hospital morgue to see what I had to do bury the guy. Dr. O'Malley said I couldn't 'claim the body' yet and alluded to the reason."

I took a deep breath. "Okay. We have to find out more about this. A lot more. But for the time being, let's not assume someone poisoned him."

"I'm not sure I even care."

"I get that. But Terry does, and if word gets out that TAT was murdered – especially if that turns out to be wrong – we'll regret the information got around."

Scoobie said nothing for several seconds.

I broke the silence by interjecting routine. "Are you staying at work, or coming home?"

"I need to stay. Couple people fell on their asses on New Year's Eve, and they're coming in for x-rays."

"Seems late."

He grunted. "I think their brains were pickled yesterday, so there was a pain delay."

I wanted to keep us talking about everyday things. "Okay. I'm getting the rest of our stuff packed, and taking Terry out with me for a while. Then we'll meet you at our place when you get off work. Is three-fifteen okay?"

"How is he?"

"Aunt Madge has been teaching him to make bread. When it comes out of the oven, we'll sample it and head to the library."

"I'm not sure guys his age want to spend time in the library."

I smiled. "Besides you, you mean?"

"I only started going there to get out of the house. Little kids can't hang around stores."

I winced. "I told him we might find out more about sports leagues or the school. He seems to want to go."

Scoobie blew out a breath. "I'm making it harder, aren't I?"

"I wouldn't be handling something like this nearly as well as you are. All I have to do is focus on Terry."

"We could have a kid, Jolie. I mean, right now."

"I know. I found someone on the Air Force base who knows him. It's good news. I'll tell you when you get home."

"Good news. I'm all for it. See you later."

I probably should have told him about the court cases, but that could wait. Instead, I sat on the edge of the bed and stared at the pale blue wall with a framed photo of seagulls on the sand.

The morning's revelations spun in my head, especially about the dismissed request for a restraining order. The medical examiner's findings could have an even bigger impact on our lives. Or at least on Terry's ability to keep recovering from his profound grief.

A drug that killed Terence? It seems so far-fetched.

I finished putting clothes in my suitcase and a duffel bag Scoobie had planned to take on our brief honeymoon at Beachcomber's Alley. Terry's partially open suitcase sat on the edge of a stuffed chair.

I stopped. Should I know his bag's contents? A parent would. *I'm not his mother. I might be his mother as of now.*

I lifted the lid, noting the *Child's Garden of Verses* atop a stack of neatly folded clothes. The brown ear of a stuffed animal poked up from one corner. I reached for it and stopped. It wasn't that I didn't want to invade his privacy as much as I probably wouldn't get it repacked the way he had it.

I shut the lid of his suitcase and zipped it.

Aunt Madge's voice came up the back staircase. "Jolie, Terry and I are having some chicken rice soup while the bread bakes. You want some?"

"Sounds good. Be down in a minute."

The bed beckoned. I had one of those all-encompassing tired feelings that came with the pregnancy. But I couldn't lie down. What did moms do if they had two kids under five and another on the way? They couldn't sleep when they wanted to.

I shut my eyes and leaned back onto the pillow, but kept one foot on the floor. After two minutes of resting, I stood. That would have to do. That and some decaf coffee. Even though it didn't have the kick of regular coffee, I always felt recharged when I had it.

Since my suitcase weighed less than Scoobie's, I picked it up and traipsed down the back stairs to the great room. Aunt Madge sat on the loveseat with her feet resting on the coffee table. Terry slept with his head in her lap.

She smiled at me and pointed to his head. "He said he would sit here until the soup was ready. Took him all of fifteen seconds to fall asleep."

I nodded and sat across from her, careful to place the suitcase on the floor without banging it. "I really appreciate this, Aunt Madge. I'm not going to dump him on you often."

She shook her head and spoke quietly. "You need to change your vocabulary. You don't want him to think he's a burden."

She was matter-of-fact, but I still flushed. "You're right, of course."

She tilted her head toward the stove. "The soup is on low. Stir it and we'll let him sleep a few minutes."

I stood. "Sure. I want him to sleep tonight."

She grinned. "You stayed with me many weekends when you were his age. I always did my best to wear you out."

TERRY LOOKED WITH INTEREST as I drove him around Ocean Alley and pointed out landmarks, stores, and schools. I explained that Ocean Alley was almost two miles long but only twelve blocks deep, with each street that parallels the ocean named for a letter of the alphabet. "Want to know why the alphabet starts with B?"

"Sure."

I sensed he was humoring me. "The Great Atlantic Hurricane removed the old boardwalk and most of 'A' Street in 1944."

"What is it called?"

"In the 1940s, they didn't name hurricanes. I guess eventually they decided they could talk about them better later if they had people names."

"We had hurricanes in Florida, but none of them came to where we were. I mean, that I remember."

"We had that big one a few years ago, Hurricane Sandy. Super Storm Sandy, I guess that's the official name."

Terry nodded. "Dad talked a lot about that. I don't remember when it happened, but a couple years ago he told me he grew up near where it came ashore. Not the worst part, though."

"Right. The part of the Jersey shore with the most severe damage is about eighty miles south of Ocean Alley." I took one hand off the wheel and pointed. "That's First Presbyterian, where the Harvest for All

Food Pantry is. It's open today, but I don't have to be there every day it's open." *Thank heavens.*

He nodded with perfunctory politeness. "And now the school?"

"Yes. It's a new building, so it's close to the edge of town." I turned away from the ocean, and in a minute we were in the driveway in front of the red brick Ocean Alley Middle School.

Terry pressed his face so close to the side window that his breath condensed on it. He pulled back. "It's kinda small. I mean, compared to my old middle school."

"I think it's about 250 kids. We can look it up online. I bet there are some pictures."

"Locked, huh?"

I nodded. "I'm sure the teachers are enjoying the break as much as the students."

He grinned. "Can we walk on the boardwalk?"

The thought made me want to nap. "Let's see, it's about thirty degrees today, and it'll be about fifteen degrees warmer tomorrow. Scoobie's off tomorrow because it's Saturday. Can you wait and do it with him?"

"Sure. You wanted to go to the library, right? Do you read a lot of books?"

"Not as many as your brother." As I said the word I realized I hadn't referred to Scoobie that way to Terry previously. I glanced at him, expecting either no reaction or a smile, and saw a tear on his cheek. "You okay?"

"Are you sure Scoobie wants to be my brother?"

As if I would say no even if I thought it. "Yes. It's a lot to get used to, for all of us, but we're happy you're here. I think you'll like Ocean Alley. And Scoobie."

"And you," he said, shyly. "And especially Aunt Madge."

I laughed. "Everybody says that."

"And the dogs." He seemed to think he might offend someone, so he added, "And Harry. Well, and everybody. The policeman was really nice to me."

"Sergeant Morehouse. Scoobie's known him for a number of years, me just a couple."

We pulled into the library parking lot.

"He's your friend, right? He went to the wedding."

"Pretty much. He also has two nephews. I haven't met them, but I think they're close to your age."

With the wind nipping our cheeks, we hustled into the library. When I went to high school junior year in Ocean Alley, the library featured drab colors and card catalogs lined the wall near the entrance. Today, the walls are vivid orange and yellow and the card catalogs are gone. A group of computers sits in the middle of the room. As always, most were occupied.

Though you can't see down the aisles of books, it's a small library. All the equipment and tables are in the main area in front of the circulation desk, and shelves of books go back about fifty feet.

Terry's gaze swept the large room. "No kids my age."

I loosened my scarf. "Let's look on the bulletin board to see what's going on this weekend."

As we ambled toward the huge cork board, Daphne looked up from the desk and smiled.

"She came to Aunt Madge's house yesterday, right?"

"Yes. She went to high school with Scoobie and me. You wouldn't have had time to see her at the wedding."

I sensed he wanted to say something, but instead he stopped in front of the bulletin board. "What's a fish fry?"

"It's a casual dinner, every Friday at St. Anthony's Parish Hall."

"Is it only fish?"

"Burgers, salads, cake. Lots of stuff."

Terry looked at me.

"I'm not sure about tonight. We can talk to Scoobie."

He nodded, and pointed. "Hey, look. There's a kids' chess club. Dad taught me to play."

I studied the flyer. Apparently they aligned their activities with the school year. No games this weekend, but the flyer noted 'drop-in play' most Saturdays, in the old bingo hall on the boardwalk. It had been turned into a community center of sorts a few years ago. Nobody wanted to play bingo if they could go to a nearby casino.

How many ten-year-olds play chess? I wondered if Scoobie did. It wouldn't surprise me, but I'd never heard him mention it.

Max's voice came from behind us. "Jolie has Terry. Terry."

Terry turned fully and gaped for a second before he closed his mouth. Max wore his antler stocking cap and a silly grin.

"Hello Max. You're right, this is Scoobie's brother Terry."

Max stuck out his hand, and Terry, looking uncertain, took it.

"Hello Scoobie's brother. I used to have a brother. A brother. Not anymore."

I suddenly remembered Max's lack of repetition when he said something about Renée, when we were in the grocery store. "I didn't know that. I'm sorry your brother is gone."

Max's smile vanished. "Gone, very gone. Sorry."

I decided to be direct with Terry. "Max had a war injury a number of years ago. We're very glad he moved here. Scoobie and I are good friends with Max. So is George. And Ramona."

Terry smiled. "Any friend of my brother's is a friend of mine."

I STARED AT THE COMPUTER SCREEN, glad that Daphne had asked Terry to help her shelve books. The library had subscriptions to many databases, so I could search obituaries that I didn't have access to at home. Marti O'Brien's came up when I keyed in Terence O'Brien's name and Panama City, Florida.

She had been born to Cuban immigrants who had braved a boat ride over tumultuous seas to reach U.S. shores in the early 1980s. Both were deceased. Any mother would worry about her children left behind. But Marti likely thought Terry had only a sixty-year old father, no one else. She must have felt frantic.

What did she think when she learned about Scoobie? Why hadn't she wanted to meet us? I realized I had no clue whether Terence told Marti about his prior marriage and son.

I pushed print, wishing there had been a photo in the obituary. Her only other media references were announcements of various Air Force promotions and such. No mention of her marriage to TAT O'Brien.

Duh. Any wedding announcement would have used her maiden name. The obituary listed her late parents' names. I found a wedding announcement in a Panama City paper that said Marti Maria Hernandez married Terence A. O'Brien eleven years ago. Terry came quickly. Then I realized she had to be almost forty when she and TAT married. They probably thought of him as a miracle baby.

I printed the brief announcements. Scoobie and I would be up all night digesting all of this.

As I stuffed the articles in my purse, Terry's giggle came from a set of shelves behind me. As I got close to them, Daphne said, "Where did you learn all that?"

"I read. A lot." He shelved a book as I turned into the aisle.

Daphne had a light frown, but she smiled. "Terry here reads as much as your husband does."

Why am I not surprised?

"So, what does my brother like to read?" Terry asked.

"Mostly fiction," Daphne said. "But if he comes across something that interests him, he'll follow his nose to any book."

Terry looked at me. "Can I check out a book?"

"Sure. On my card today?" I asked Daphne.

She nodded. "We can fill out the form for Terry to get one. It'll be mailed to you."

Terry almost skipped away from us. "I know what I want."

I shrugged at Daphne. "We'll probably need more shelves." I lowered my voice. "He's smart, right?"

Daphne nodded. "You and I are smart. He's Scoobie smart."

CHAPTER EIGHTEEN

I'D NEVER SEEN MY HUSBAND so distracted. He barely took any pleasure in introducing our pet skunk, Pebbles, to Terry. Usually that's a staged event that includes wandering the house looking for her, with a guest gingerly peering into corners or behind the couch.

Pebbles is only in one place when we have company – under our bed. Jazz slips under the dust ruffle to visit her periodically. After a guest's search, Scoobie would eventually announce that Jazz had found our recalcitrant skunk.

Tonight, he guided Terry straight to our bedroom, where Terry lay splayed on his stomach, head under the bed, trying to coax out Pebbles. Jazz sat on his butt.

As soon as Terry's head vanished, I hugged Scoobie, hard, and whispered, "We'll get it all figured out."

He leaned into me and relaxed, but only so much. In a low voice, he said, "Wish we knew more now, but we don't." In a normal volume, he said, "You mentioned good news?"

Terry's muffled voice reached us. "Does she bite?"

Scoobie knelt next to the bed. "We've never tested her teeth. Why don't you come on out? We'll fix some dinner. When she gets used to you, she'll wander out."

Dinner? I had almost no food in the house. With the wedding looming, I'd focused on food for guests, not our pantry. I looked down at Scoobie as he slid Terry out by his shoes. "We may need to order in."

Terry stood brush off his pants, which had acquired a couple of dust balls. Or a wad of cat hair. "What about the fish fry?"

Scoobie raised an eyebrow at me. I knew it would be a good way for Terry to meet kids, but no way could I stay awake that long. Not without a nap. I shrugged.

"Terry, you and I are going, and we'll bring the pregnant lady some carry-out food."

"That's okay with Jolie?"

"She's not the boss of me."

I shook my head as Terry seemed unsure whether we were joking around or having an argument. "You'll have to get used to your brother's weird humor. Truthfully, I need a nap. Pregnant women are often especially tired during the first trimester."

Terry cocked his head. "So, you were pregnant before you got married?"

Damn. Who'd have thought I'd have to answer that question?

When I was five, one of my babysitters got married and had a baby a few weeks later. I sort of remembered people saying that it took a long time to "grow a baby."

When I asked her about this, Aunt Madge replied that, "First babies are special, they don't take nine months." A perfect answer to a five-year old's question, and a wonderful perspective.

But not one I could use here. For all I knew, Terry had learned the birds and the bees on his school playground. Or by watching cable.

"Yes," Scoobie began.

I interjected with a slight fib. "We had already planned to get married, we just hadn't made it official." *Not a lie, we were heading in that direction.*

Terry's brow furrowed. "So, the baby made it official?"

Scoobie wiggled his eyebrows at me, á la Groucho Marx. "Just moved it up a month or so. You get to be a..." He stopped.

I smiled. "An uncle, but more like a brother, sort of."

Terry seemed perplexed. "Will I share a room with the baby?"

Scoobie squeezed his shoulders and propelled Terry toward the front door. "We'll have to start house hunting. Meanwhile," he pointed into the second bedroom, "you'll get that futon and some drawers."

Terry glanced at Scoobie's hands on his shoulders. "Okay. So, you're pushing me to the fish fry?""

Scoobie leaned closer and kissed me as they sort of duck-walked by. "Yep." His expression grew serious. "Rest. If you need stuff done, Terry and I'll handle it."

I nodded. "When you come back, bring in the suitcases that are in my car."

"Please," Terry said.

As he grabbed their coats, Scoobie flashed a grin at Terry. "We'll have to teach her some manners."

When the door shut behind them, I almost ran to the sofa to lie down. But I couldn't sleep. Instead, my eyes roamed our small bungalow. It would take a while to get into a new house, regardless of whether we could afford it.

The large area that served as the living and dining rooms ran the full length of our bungalow. With Aunt Madge's guidance, I had just finished making matching, light green curtains for windows at the front and back of the airy room.

Because there had been only two of us, we had a two-person table just outside the kitchen. It did have a small leaf underneath it, and we could get another dining chair.

Our galley kitchen had a table more like TV tray size. We could eat most meals in the dining area, but Terry could do after-school snacks in the kitchen.

Having one bathroom would be a manageable challenge, but I'd have to remember to be fully clothed when I applied makeup. I could clear off a shelf in the linen closet so Terry had some space of his own. *Kids don't have a lot of bathroom stuff.* I giggled.

A black streak landed on my chest. "Oomph. Jazz!"

She took only two seconds to settle onto my chest and head-butt my chin. "Okay, okay, I get it. You're establishing that you reign in this domain." I scratched the top of her head. "What do you think, girl? When you and I came to Ocean Alley, we lived in a bedroom at the Cozy Corner. Now we have a husband, a kid, another on the way, and a house. Soon a bigger house."

She yawned widely.

"Ugh. You have cat breath."

She head-butted my chin again.

"Enough. You want the floor?"

Jazz flopped on one side, her sleeping posture when she wants to use me as a bed.

My position on the couch let my eyes travel to the small hallway with the two bedrooms that opened into it. The one Scoobie and I used was a decent size, but the one that would now be Terry's was barely ten-by-ten. We could maybe squeeze in a small chest of drawers. Too bad no one had garage sales in January.

I wondered whether Terence had left any life insurance for Terry. Maybe we could use a little of it for a new chest, so he didn't feel he was only worth second-hand furniture. Would we be able to save money for him for college? Good heavens. I was thinking like a mom.

WHY WAS SCOOBIE TRYING to tell me a secret? Something about Terry? I opened my eyes.

Terry repeated, in a whisper, "Wake up, sleepyhead."

Scoobie stood behind where Terry knelt next to the sofa, smiling. "Hungry?"

"Ravenous."

Terry grinned and looked at Scoobie as he stood. "Should we tell her who we met?"

Scoobie opened the top of a brown sack and waved it under my nose. It smelled heavenly. "You can tell her."

I sat up. "You can tell me while I eat."

"Brought several things. You want to sit at the table?"

I sat up and nodded to Terry. "Good idea. Who did you see?"

He ticked names off on his fingers. "Aunt Madge and Uncle Harry. And George. Oh, George said I should tell you you're a…" he glanced at Scoobie.

"Slacker."

I snorted.

"Slacker," Terry continued. "And Sergeant Morehouse was there with his sister and she has two boys. One is only eight, but the one named Kevin is eleven. He said I can watch his soccer practice. But I have to talk to the coach about whether I can be on the team right away. Even if I can't, I can probably practice with them."

He took a breath and I grinned at him. "That's a lot of people to see at one dinner." I sat at the table and peered into the bag. "Yum. Grilled fish sandwich."

Terry sat next to me. "You had a couple more French fries when we started for home."

He called this home. "I don't need a whole lot of extra calories."

His expression grew serious. "But you're eating for two. When Mrs. Booker was pregnant, she said that meant she could have a milkshake every day."

I thought Francis Booker said he and his wife had no children. I must have frowned, because Terry added, "I keep thinking you know everyone I do. They're from Florida. My Mom," his voice warbled briefly, "and Mr. Booker repaired helicopters together."

No time like the present. "I waited until we were all three together to tell you I talked to Francis Booker today."

Scoobie's questioning look accompanied the glass of water he handed me, but he let Terry ask the questions.

"That's good. Did my Dad give you their phone number? Oh, wait. You didn't talk to Dad, right?"

"I did not. Aunt Madge would call it a happy coincidence. I called the base to, uh, see if I needed to tell anyone about your dad. Francis works in…"

"The Community Relations Office. He helped us because he was Mom's friend, but he said he would've helped even if he didn't know her." He stopped and pressed his lips together.

"He said he and your mom, Marti, were good friends. And apparently his wife Linda makes cookies you like."

"With M&Ms in them. Dad said he would call them when we got settled. He said they would mail us some boxes. Of our stuff. That didn't fit in our suitcases."

"Ah. He didn't mention that. I'll have to give him our address."

Terry frowned, thinking. "I don't know if Dad told him before. We packed the boxes and left them in our living room. And I think, I think there might be one in the trunk."

Their car. Where is the car? I needed to remember to ask Scoobie if he knew.

Scoobie cleared his throat. "Mr. and Mrs. Booker must be good friends. Only really good friends help with a move."

"Yep." He sighed. "I'm going to miss them." His lips quivered.

I exchanged a look with Scoobie. "When we plan your dad's service, would you like them to be there?"

Terry's face brightened and then grew serious. "I would like it a lot. But in the Air Force, you have to put in for leave a long time before. Unless it's an emergency. Like, um, like," his eyes filled, "like cancer."

Scoobie handed him one of my napkins. "You can cry, you know."

Terry accepted it and wiped each cheek. "Crying makes me feel worse."

"I hear you." Scoobie looked at me. "What else did you learn, sleuth of mine?"

I wrinkled my nose at him. "Francis said…"

"I'm pretty sure he'd tell you to call him Frank."

I nodded at Terry. "In fact, he did. Frank said he and Linda would try to come up for your dad's funeral. I didn't want to say yes until we talked to you."

Terry put his arms on the table, placed his head on them and began to cry. Hard. Between sobs, he said, "I miss Dad, but I miss Frank and Linda, too."

Scoobie knelt next to him before I could move. "Then we'll have to make sure to invite them often." He looked at me, more or less in desperation.

"Of course." I pushed more napkins toward Terry. "And it would not be right away, but sometime we can take a vacation in Florida."

Terry's blotched face rose from his crossed arms. "Really?"

Scoobie and I both said, "Sure." Scoobie added, "You may have moved, but that doesn't mean you lose your friends."

Terry sniffed and took another napkin. His face and eyes were red, but he also seemed calmer than a guy who just finished crying. He'd learned to absorb a lot.

"It's Frank and Linda I miss. They said I can call them by their first names." He looked at Scoobie. "Do you have email?"

Scoobie threw back his head and laughed. "Jolie uses computers more than I do. She'll set you up."

Terry wiped his cheeks with the back of one hand. "I have an account. Can we email Frank and Linda?"

TERRY WENT TO SLEEP WITH a smile. I had called Frank to tell him he was about to get an email. The couple emailed back and forth with Terry for an hour, until one of them, Linda I thought, announced bedtime.

They even knew when he went to bed. He must have spent a lot of time with them. My thoughts went back to Frank saying they had no children, and Terry mentioning a pregnancy. Had they lost a child? I couldn't stand to think about that.

I cocked my ear to listen to Scoobie talking on the phone with Frank. He'd started the conversation with honesty about his lack of contact with TAT – I had to stop thinking that way, or I'd say it in front of Terry – and then done a lot of listening.

Scoobie paced through the kitchen and living room, and joined me again on the sofa as he continued the conversation. "I can't tell you how great it is to talk to someone who knew them well." More listening. "Okay, well we aren't in a big rush. Why don't you check and call us when you know whether you can come?"

I couldn't quite hear Frank, but I caught something about driving. Scoobie frowned lightly as Frank said more.

"It's hard to know for sure," Scoobie replied. "But he seems to be handling it as well as any ten-year-old could."

Scoobie listened again and raised his eyebrows at me. "Sure. We have a really small place, but I'm sure you could stay with Jolie's Aunt Madge." He smiled as he listened for a few seconds. "Good to know he has a favorite."

CHAPTER NINETEEN

TERRY GOT HIS FIRST invitation Saturday morning. Morehouse's nephew called to see if Terry wanted to watch their soccer practice. He did.

After Scoobie left to drive to the practice field with Terry, I focused on tidying the house and thinking about how to arrange our second bedroom so it looked like a child's room rather than a catch-all spare space that happened to have a futon.

My thoughts drifted to what I'd learned in court records. I told Scoobie I had found some 'interesting' information, but we were both dead on our feet last night. I supposed parents expected exhaustion. Priorities we had before kids realigned to meet the need for sleep.

Before kids. BK. I smiled.

Scoobie came home as I finished breakfast dishes. "Hello bride."

I smiled. "In the kitchen."

He sat at the kitchen table. "We have at least two kid-free hours. Is this how parents measure time?"

I wiped my hands on a towel. "Probably. At least we have a few months with no diapers."

He sighed. "I guess we should talk about what you found out yesterday. While we won't get interrupted."

I nodded. "Let's get comfy on the couch."

He kissed my cheek. "Must be good."

It only took me two minutes to outline the arrest records. "But that wasn't the most surprising part."

"From what my mother always said, arrests would be no surprise at all."

Explaining the restraining order was harder. I could tell Scoobie's reaction was the same as mine. How could his father leave him with a woman Terence O'Brien clearly feared?

He stared without speaking, and entered the kitchen. He came out and looked intently at me. "What the hell was he thinking?"

"I wish I had an answer for you. Maybe...I mean that one altercation led to some kind of mental health treatment."

Scoobie snorted. "Probably code for alcohol rehab."

Before Scoobie could say anything else, the phone rang. Scoobie glanced at the caller ID. "Aunt Madge." He lifted the receiver and handed it to me.

"Hi, Aunt Madge."

"I knew Terry was going to watch soccer practice, so I thought this might be a good time."

I shrugged at Scoobie and he nodded. "Sure. What's up?"

"Arnie got the security tapes reviewed. You know, from the night before your wedding."

I gestured that Scoobie should come closer, and pushed the speaker button. "Okay. Scoobie's here, too."

"The camera captured the area around the door and cash register, so you two aren't initially visible. But Terence and Terry sat in a booth by the door."

"Right," I said. "Scoobie's back was to them, but I saw them."

"If I had to guess, as Terence was leaving, he recognized Scoobie. His expression changed, and he moved a lot faster to get Terry out of there."

"Makes no sense," Scoobie said, "if he was bringing him to us."

"It did several minutes later. You and Jolie had left by then. You were on the tape heading out the door. Terence came back. He looked toward your booth, and then around the diner. When he didn't see you two, he left."

"Coming back to talk to Scoobie, you think?" I asked.

"It certainly looked that way."

Scoobie did an exaggerated shrug, and then seemed to realize Aunt Madge couldn't see him. "I'm not sure how knowing this helps."

"It may not," Aunt Madge said. "I think it simply lends credence to the idea that he may have meant to talk to you before the wedding."

"But no Terry with him?" I asked.

"No. The Budget Motel was close. He must have dropped him off and come back."

When neither of us said anything, she continued. "Arnie has a DVD of the time period, but I don't know that it will tell you more."

"Thanks, Aunt Madge. More to process," I said.

Scoobie nodded. "Thanks for following through. Glad I didn't have to."

We hung up, and Scoobie again moved to the kitchen and back. "You know, when we get a bigger house I'll have more room to pace. Let's go for a walk. It's above freezing."

"That sounds great. I think my gloves are in my car. I'll grab them on the way out."

He took my dark blue parka from the coat tree and held it open. I slid into the arms and zipped the front before turning toward him.

Scoobie's expression was, well, expressionless, but when my eyes met his he forced a grim smile. "It'll be okay."

He grabbed his coat from the back of a chair. I put my keys in my jacket pocket and left the house ahead of him.

As we neared the car, he moved to the passenger side. "Let's drive to the boardwalk and hike there."

"Sure."

I drove toward the ocean and easily found a parking space near the wooden stairs that led to the elevated walk. We didn't speak during the drive, but it wasn't a stressful silence. I wanted to talk more about his father's possible murder, but I'd learned that if my husband didn't have much to say, he kept quiet. He didn't need to talk aloud to process his thoughts.

As we climbed the steps, I thought about how I'd met Scoobie the second time on the boardwalk, not far from where we were to start our stroll. He'd been adding tape to worn sneakers and I hadn't recognized him until he spoke.

Scoobie took my hand. "You called me 'sir' the first time we met up again."

"That's so weird. I was just thinking about how you were taping your shoes."

He laughed. "A lifetime ago."

The smell of French fries greeted us. Even in the depth of winter, the French fry place opened on weekends. "You want some?" Scoobie asked.

"Maybe after we walk."

Most of the brightly colored, clapboard stores were shuttered against the cold salt air. The cotton candy store owner had scraped some of the pink paint from the trim around the doors and windows. He alternated the building's pastel shades from yellow to blue to pink.

I looked at my husband's profile. "Deep thoughts?"

He squeezed my hand. "Yeah. Not really a lot to say. I get that he would be afraid of my mom. But why leave me?" He looked hard at the roiling surf, then glanced at me. "What I really don't get is why he didn't come back later."

I took my hand from his and tightened my scarf. "Especially after he had Terry."

"Guilt, maybe."

"Probably." I put my hand back into his. "That and not wanting to confess to Marti that he had left...Hey, I wonder if he had a will?"

Scoobie shook his head. "I don't think we know."

"We'll probably be able to find some records somewhere. Maybe even the funeral home has ways to look."

"That's a good idea." Scoobie slowed his pace. "I'm sorry, was I going too fast?"

I smiled. "Pregnant women are supposed to get a lot of exercise."

He grunted. "This has been so all-absorbing I even forgot you were pregnant for, like, two hours."

"I can't." My tone was more serious than I'd intended.

Scoobie stopped and faced me. "You aren't sor...?"

"Of course not. Just waiting for month four so I won't be so tired."

"Oh, right." He looked behind him. "We're almost to Java Jolt. Want some tea or something?"

I didn't want tea, I'd just have to pee before we got home. I did want to get warm. "Sure."

We quickened our pace and reached the coffee shop in less than a minute. As soon as the door shut behind us my nose began to run. I grabbed a napkin from the counter and blew.

From her spot behind the serving counter, Megan laughed. "Good day to open your sinuses. Hello you two."

We were the only customers in the small shop, so as Scoobie took off his stocking cap he bowed. "Me lady."

I groaned and Megan said, "Oh, no. You're planning another Talk Like a Pirate Day fundraiser for the food pantry."

Scoobie grinned broadly. "Megan, what a great idea! Isn't it, darling?"

I stuck my tongue out at him. "You just want to wield that rubber sword."

Megan reached under the counter and pulled out two mugs, which she placed on the counter. "Tea is on the house."

"We couldn't," I began.

"Did you bring money?" Scoobie asked.

"Crud."

Megan laughed. "You just got married. If you think I'd charge you, you're nuts."

I took off my coat and looked around. "You've painted the walls a lighter color." I realized that she had also replaced some of the dark-colored tables with a mix of round tables in a light oak veneer.

"Yep. Alicia and I are planning more of a seashore theme than Joe had." She stepped back from the counter so I could see that her light yellow, canvas-type apron. It sported a beach scene, complete with shells, below the waist.

"Very nice."

Scoobie brought the mugs and one peppermint teabag to the table. Neither of us likes strong tea.

I gestured to Megan. "Can you sit with us for a couple of minutes?"

"Sure." Before she came to the customer side she gently shook the thermos of coffee that sat on the counter, probably making sure there was enough coffee. Local customers are on the honor system in the winter. Of course, since we'd brought no money, we wouldn't throw any in the large sugar bowl next to the coffee pot.

We filled our cups with hot water from the second thermos on the counter, and I added honey.

As we sat, Megan looked at Scoobie. "Madge called. She said he does kind of look like you at the same age."

Scoobie raised his eyebrows. "Aunt Madge is passing gossip?"

Megan shrugged. "Not gossip if it's true. Plus, she said she wanted me to know the scoop in case I heard people making up stuff."

I laughed. "Sounds like her."

"He is cute," Megan said.

Scoobie nodded. "And he seems to be a really good kid. He's lost both his parents, and he doesn't wallow in it."

Together, Megan and I said, "He has you."

Scoobie added, "Us."

I took the teabag from my mug and passed it to Scoobie on a spoon. "We don't know a lot about him yet. He's expecting us to enroll him in middle school this week, and I don't even know what kind of student he is."

"The school here can help you get his transcripts." Megan turned to Scoobie. "If there's a funeral, do you want people there?"

Scoobie shook his head gently, seemingly conveying a lack of opinion more than a negative one. "I like to see my friends, and Terry would probably like it. And," he brightened, "a family he knew in Florida may come up."

Megan lifted her eyebrows. "Long way to go for a funeral."

Scoobie nodded. "It sounds as if they spent a fair bit of time with Terry after his mom died."

I frowned slightly. "It would sure be nice if we had an idea who Terence knew when he lived here."

"And we care why?" Scoobie asked.

"Not for us, for Terry. Maybe someone would remember something good about him and speak when the minister asks...damn. Are we going to ask Reverend Jamison to lead a service?"

Scoobie shrugged. "I have zero energy to plan anything." Our eyes met. "Let's ask Aunt Madge."

I nodded.

Megan's expression looked puzzled. "Father Teehan knew him."

Scoobie spit tea back into his mug, and his eyes watered. "You're kidding."

Megan seemed flustered. "I'm sorry, Father Teehan came by this morning. I shouldn't have said anything."

Scoobie's laugh was humorless. "Please. I'm open to hearing whatever anyone knows."

"You want me to talk to him?" I asked.

Scoobie eyed his mug. "Would you?"

"Sure."

"You want fresh tea?" Megan asked.

"Nah. It's my own germs."

The papers I gathered at the courthouse moved to the front of my thought process again. I hadn't thought to mention the name of the lawyer who represented TAT. "You know, a lawyer had to handle the divorce filing. I can try to find that person." *I could mention I already thought I knew. Or not.*

Scoobie shrugged. "I suppose the person could still be here." He brightened. "It might shed some light on..." He stopped.

"A bunch of stuff." I hoped knowing more didn't make things worse.

The door opened and two couples almost blew into the coffee shop. Megan got up to serve them.

We sat in silence for several seconds. I lifted my tea to sip. "Guess it's hard to clear your head when we keep talking about it all."

"It's okay. Not like it'll go away. Besides, if I can deal with him just showing up and dying on our wedding night, I can deal with anything."

I patted his hand. "You always can."

He nodded. "I'm definitely better equipped than I would have been a few years ago."

"I don't mind having Terry."

He smiled. "I know. He sure seems smart."

I remembered Daphne's comment. "We'll probably have our hands full."

"We'll have to…" Scoobie began.

The door banged open and Lester Argrow came in, preceded by the smell of his perpetual cigar. It always hangs unlit from his mouth in public places.

He grinned broadly. "Great. I was gonna look for you two in a day or two. You know, after the honeymoon, or whatever it is now." He approached the counter.

I leaned toward Scoobie's ear and spoke softly. "We can leave."

"We'll give him a couple minutes."

Scoobie has never been fond of Lester, but they tolerate each other. Since he's Ramona's uncle, we have to. I actually like him. He's funny.

Lester pulled up a chair, swung it backwards to sit, and dumped four packets of sugar into his black coffee. As he began to stir, he looked at Scoobie. "Does the kid play soccer? Lots of soccer teams in town."

"He went over to watch a…" Scoobie began.

"Cause soccer, it has a lot of equipment. You know, balls, special shoes. You might need even more than three bedrooms."

I laughed aloud, and Scoobie, who had at first frowned, grinned. "You never change, Lester."

"I sniff out the best deals in town," he said.

I grew serious. "I know we talked to you about maybe getting something bigger, but we probably need to reevaluate our finances first. You know, now that we're three."

"How much Social Security does the kid get?"

Scoobie and I looked at each other, not understanding Lester's point.

Lester slurped coffee. "See, since his dad, your dad, died, Social Security pays something every month 'til the kid's like, I dunno, eighteen, I think."

Scoobie looked as stunned as I felt.

Lester looked from me to Scoobie. "You didn't know?"

We shook our heads.

"You know the old guy's Social Security number?"

"I don't think so," Scoobie said.

Lester shrugged. "Be on his Medicare card. Or Peters can find it for you."

Lester pulled out his smartphone and punched the screen a few times before sliding to a photo of a two-story house. "See, this here on Conch..."

I shook my head. "One level, or maybe a Cape Cod style. They usually have two bedrooms on the first floor."

"And what, you rent the top floor?"

Scoobie deadpanned. "There's a rumor going around that I have more siblings."

Lester's cigar fell out of his mouth. "No sh..kidding. Damn. I mean, could be good people." He stopped as Scoobie grinned.

Lester grunted as he retrieved his cigar from the table top and took a tiny black and white notepad from a pants pocket. "Shoulda figured. So, bedrooms on the first floor. What else?"

A glance at Scoobie told me house hunting would be too much to consider today. "I think Scoobie and I, and Terry, need to talk about that first. Won't be this week."

Lester downed the second half of his cup of coffee in one slurp. "Okay, you think. I'll keep my eyes open, but I won't pester you for a week."

After he left, Scoobie half-smiled. "A no-pester Lester. I could almost like the guy."

CHAPTER TWENTY

AS WE FINISHED OUR TEA, Scoobie's phone jingled. He pulled it from the back pocket of his jeans and glanced at the caller ID. "Morehouse."

"Scoobie. Sergeant Morehouse here."

"Hey, thanks for having your nephew call to invite Terry to soccer practice."

Scoobie tilted his phone so I could listen. Morehouse's words were rushed. "Told him to ask, but also that he don't have to invite him another time unless he wants to."

"Makes sense."

"So, listen. The ME sent over her report on your father. She also said she told you she thought it might notta been natural causes."

"Actually," Scoobie winked at me, "she flat out said she thought somebody poisoned him."

"And she's doin' more tests. Readin' the report, I'm not convinced."

155

"I could imagine people willing to plot his murder."

"Have it your way. All I'm sayin' is it coulda been an accident. You know, him forgetting he took some pills and taking another dose later."

I couldn't tell what Scoobie thought about this. I liked the idea, if only because Terry wouldn't have to think about his father as a murder victim. He'd already had his life turned upside down.

"What kind of pills?" Scoobie asked.

"I don't suppose you know what kind of medicine your old man took."

Scoobie tapped a teaspoon on the table for a second. "Terry might, but I'd rather not ask him. Didn't Dana say she brought my father's suitcase or something to your office?"

"Yeah. I got it under my desk, to give to you. You care if I go through it?"

"Sure. We can split any money you find."

"From the age of his car and suitcase, I'm not expectin' any."

Scoobie and I looked at each other. "Where's the car?" he asked.

"Impound lot. No charge, but you'll probably need to get it by Monday or there will be."

"Swell," Scoobie said.

I remembered thinking I needed to ask Scoobie about the car. The thought had flown from my mind when Terry began crying. I leaned toward the phone. "What drug do you think he had too much of?"

Morehouse snorted. "Figured Scoobie was alone or you'da butted in before now."

I used my sweetest tone. "Nice to talk to you, too."

"Uh huh. Digitalis."

Scoobie's eyebrows went up. "The heart drug? You're saying maybe he took an extra dose?"

"He didn't have a prescription for it."

Scoobie frowned. "You just asked me if I knew what drugs he took. Now you're telling me you know."

My question exactly.

Morehouse said nothing for several seconds. "I gotta ask you questions the way I would ask any family member. On any case."

Scoobie's words were clipped. "For the record, I neither know, nor care, what meds he took."

"Scoobie," I began.

"I hear ya," Morehouse said. "He had a pill bottle in one pocket. Led us to his pharmacy. I don't want to question the kid. But you gotta find a way to ask him what illnesses your old man had besides the cancer. It could take a while to get medical records."

"I don't even know what kind of cancer he had."

Another pause. "Let me drop off a copy of the ME report. I'll swing by your house tomorrow, unless you need it tonight." He hung up.

Scoobie looked at me. "I keep waiting for the final shoe to drop, but I think it's going to be a number like Imelda Marcos' collection." He pocketed the phone.

I shrugged. "Sorry I can't take some of the load for you."

He grinned, briefly. "I told you about that saying sorry stuff."

"What would digitalis do to a person? If they took too much, I mean."

"We had a course on drug interactions, but my knowledge is pretty basic. I know it can make you sick to your stomach, extra drowsy."

"So, if it's a heart drug, what would too much do to the heart?"

Scoobie shook his head from side to side, apparently weighing his response. "It can do a number on heart rhythm. Arrhythmia, it's called. That's bad for anyone, but especially for someone weak from another illness."

I blew a breath. "Terry has a suitcase sitting open on the desk in the spare room. Why don't you go through it with him? Maybe it'll give you a chance to talk about...whatever."

Scoobie shrugged. "I will because I want to get to know him better. I'm not going to ask leading questions."

I smiled. "You sound like a cop show."

"God help me."

TERRY WAS STILL WITH Morehouse's nephew when we got home, so Scoobie and I rearranged his room. We emptied a two-drawer file cabinet so he could use the drawers, and Scoobie put the files in plastic bags and stuck them under our bed.

"Does Pebbles eat paper?" I asked.

"Only tax files."

"Funny. Let's move that box of your textbooks to the attic."

"Sure." He opened the lid on the copy paper box and quickly went through the books. "I'll keep out the medical dictionary. There's plenty of material at work if I have radiology-type questions."

I flattened the futon. "Let's keep it in sleeping mode, so it's more like a real bed."

A car door slammed in the driveway and I walked to the front door. A happy looking Terry waved goodbye to the car's occupants and started toward the porch. He saw me and grinned. "We went for pizza."

I held the door open. "Do I owe anyone money?"

He shook his head. "Mrs. Downey said next time Scoobie's buying."

I laughed. "Sounds like a plan. Come in and see what we're doing to your room."

His brows knitted. "Did I leave a mess?"

"Of course not. We wanted to make it more like a bedroom and less like an office."

I started to follow him to the bedroom, but my cell chirped. Caller ID showed Frank Booker. I let Terry and Scoobie go ahead of me.

"Jolie? Frank and Linda here."

"Good to hear from you."

"Listen," he paused, "I strung together leave starting today through Thursday."

I quickly considered timeframes for funeral planning. "Are you driving or flying?"

"I think driving. In one of Terry's emails, he said he wanted us to pick up some boxes his dad had in the living room." He chuckled. "We went over there today. I think we can fit them all in our Toyota."

I hadn't realized Terry had passed his request directly to Frank, but I supposed he didn't have to go through Scoobie or me.

"That's really good of you, but isn't that a lot of driving awfully quickly?"

"We'll spell each other. Can you really do the funeral on short notice?

"We can aim for Tuesday. I'll talk to Terry and Scoobie."

"What?" Frank seemed to be saying something to his wife

"Jolie? It's Linda. Would you tell Terry I'll bring ingredients for his favorite cookies?"

I almost felt a pang of jealousy. "I will. You'll have to share your recipe."

"Oh, sure." Her tone lacked enthusiasm.

Terry came out of the bedroom like a miniature rocket. "Is that Linda? Can I talk to her?"

I handed him the phone and went to what I now thought of as Terry's room to talk to Scoobie.

As Scoobie put a sheet on the futon I grabbed a corner and tucked it in. "So, they'll be here for a Tuesday funeral. I better talk to Aunt Madge."

"I think it'll be good for Terry. I'll talk to Peters tomorrow, and George can help me get something in the paper."

I shrugged. "The funeral home will do that." We added the top sheet. "If they are this fond of Terry, they might want a continuing relationship."

"You think there's something wrong with that?"

I took a blanket Scoobie had brought in from the linen closet. "Probably not. I guess I want us to help Terry make decisions, or whatever. I don't want us to be challenged."

Scoobie stopped smoothing the blanket. "What makes you say that? We haven't even met them."

How could I explain that it was Linda's tone of voice when I asked her to share a recipe? I had immediately thought she wanted to maintain an upper hand. Maybe she saw Terry as a replacement for the child she had not been able to have.

"Jolie?"

"I'm sorry. Brain freeze. Nothing in particular, I guess. I think we'll have a lot of big decisions in the next few months. Hard enough with three people in the equation."

He grinned. "Throw in Aunt Madge's advice while you're at it."

Terry came into the room, phone at his ear and an ear-to-ear smile. "They're coming." He handed the phone to me. "They want to talk to you again."

Frank asked if I really meant that they could stay at the Cozy Corner. Though I hadn't asked Aunt Madge yet, I said yes. If she didn't like the idea, Scoobie and I could pay for a room at Beachcomber's Alley.

As I hung up, I gave myself a talking to. What if Frank and Linda Booker did want to stay in touch with Terry? I didn't mind having him, but it would be a big adjustment. With a baby, you didn't get any sleep, but you also made all the decisions for the child.

Pleasant as he seemed, we would butt heads with Terry sometimes. It was part of growing up.

I decided to be delighted that Terry could have a Florida extended family to visit. Who knew? When Terry turned fifteen or so, maybe I'd even welcome it.

CHAPTER TWENTY-ONE

ON SUNDAY EVENING, I stretched on the couch while Scoobie and Terry put together a chest of drawers we'd bought at Walmart. The chest was not large. Terry's suitcase had only a few outfits, some books, and a plastic container that now held the last one of Linda Booker's M&M cookies. Apparently he'd been hoarding them.

We had met with Father Teehan in the afternoon. I used the meeting as an excuse to tell Renée not to bring the girls down. I wanted Terry to spend time with them, but I just couldn't do one more thing I didn't absolutely have to do.

Renée's frame of mind matched mine. She was already juggling their schedules so she could bring Julia down for the funeral.

Renée and Andrew deemed Michelle too young. As gracious as Andrew had been, I knew he probably preferred staying in Lakewood with his youngest daughter.

Terry loved talking to someone who knew 'our Dad,' as he always said. Father Teehan had known Terence as a parishioner, and he didn't pretend they were good friends. That didn't bother Terry.

Father Teehan agreed to do the service when Terry said that he and his mom had gone to church every Sunday, and his dad went on Christmas and Easter.

"You're talking about half of the Catholics I know," Father Teehan had joked. Thankfully, he agreed to conduct the service at the funeral home.

I didn't care about the type of service, but Scoobie really didn't want a full Catholic Mass. "There's no way I can sit through an hour of a church service that honors my Father."

I mostly didn't want to do the kneeling stuff. Plus, I had to think about raising a kid Catholic. That would be different. Maybe we could get him to like First Prez. I immediately felt guilty for not wanting to have to go to two churches.

Even a simple funeral service takes a lot of planning. The funeral home could accommodate us Tuesday afternoon, and they made arrangements to bury Terence in a national cemetery, though not for several days. Apparently the cemetery asked you to wait when they were backed up.

This confused Terry, so Mr. Peters simply told him that if the cemetery had a lot of requests for the same day, they tried to schedule things so the people who came from out of town got priority. I had no idea if that was true, but it appeased Terry.

If we had been paying for all of it ourselves, we might have had to go with cremation. Given what I'd learned earlier from Frank Booker, that could be tough for Terry.

Thanks to Bill Oliver's generosity, the funeral home costs and transportation to the cemetery would be covered. Since he wouldn't take money, we'd have to think of another way to repay him. Maybe if we needed dentures when we were old...Wait. He was a pediatric dentist. Oh well, we could take Terry.

Scoobie's Bible sat on my lap. I had surmised that Terry wanted to choose the verses with his brother, so the two O'Brien boys had selected three and wanted my approval. As if I would object to anything they picked.

I recognized the one that began, "The Lord is my Shepherd." They were probably the same in any Bible. One passage caught my eye. "Surely your goodness and love will follow me all the days of my life, and I will dwell in the house of the Lord forever." Terry probably saw his dad as having goodness and love.

Between the wedding and this funeral, I'll hear more prayers than I usually do in a couple of months.

The brothers had just returned to the living room when the doorbell rang. Scoobie raised an eyebrow as he stood. "Expecting anyone?"

"Nope."

Terry, as seemed to be his wont, followed his brother to the door.

"Come in Sergeant," Scoobie said.

Morehouse entered, and Terry pointed to the suitcase in his hand. "That's my Dad's."

I sat up and gestured to the rocking chair across from the couch. "Would you like some coffee or tea?"

"You okay?" he asked.

"Fine. I lie down when I get a chance." I nodded at Terry. "I now have a second person to bring me what I need."

Terry grinned and sat next to me. Morehouse took the rocker across from us, and Scoobie sat on the arm of the couch.

Morehouse nodded at Terry as he placed the suitcase on the floor next to his chair. "It's your dad's case. The night of the wedding we took it back to the police station to keep for a couple of days."

Terry frowned. "Did you look in it?"

Before Scoobie could say he'd given permission, Morehouse said, "Just briefly. We looked for medicine, so we could tell the hospital what he took."

Terry's expression cleared. "Good idea. But I get to keep it now, right?"

"Right," Scoobie said. "We can unpack it later if you like."

Morehouse smiled. "It seemed as if your dad liked books as much as your brother." He paused, then continued. "Because your dad was by himself when he…"

"Plowed into the light pole?"

My eyes widened and Scoobie said, "Who did you hear say that?"

Terry shrugged. "I heard George say that to somebody."

I'll kill him.

Scoobie's tone was dry. "I'll have to tell him to use more respectful terminology."

Morehouse cleared his throat. "Since he didn't regain consciousness after that, we had to do a little investigating."

Terry frowned and looked at Scoobie before turning back to Morehouse. "You didn't cut him up, did you?"

"Mostly blood tests," Morehouse said. "It's not always like crime cra...shows on TV."

I knew the ME had done more than that, but was relieved that Morehouse chose not to be specific. No little kid wanted to hear that his father had been autopsied the way television shows depict it.

"There's one thing you can help me with," Morehouse continued.

Terry's face showed reluctance. "Uh, okay."

Morehouse pulled a three-by-five card from his pocket. "This here's a list of his medicines." He held it up, but didn't hold it close to Terry. "Looks as if he had one thing designed to slow his cancer..."

"Txandi," Terry said.

"Damn," Scoobie said. Then as Terry stared at him, he added, "Lots of kids your age don't know what their parents take."

Terry grinned. "I helped put out his pills if he was tired."

"Good job," I added, not recognizing the drug, or probably how to spell it.

Terry sobered. "It's for when the other prostate cancer medicine stops working." His eyes filled and he wiped one hand over them before looking at Morehouse again.

"Right" Morehouse said. "One of the unusual side effects can be seizures, which may be why your dad stopped steerin' his car."

"Huh." Terry frowned. "Maybe if I didn't ask dad to get me that apple pie..."

Scoobie shook his head forcefully. "The two things are unrelated. Wherever Terence, Dad, was at that time, he could've...drifted off."

Terry looked at me.

I nodded. "I hate to think of you in that car."

He whispered, "Maybe I could have grabbed the steering wheel."

Morehouse interjected. "And maybe you would have grabbed it so hard you went into another car instead of the pole. I learned one thing in this job." He pointed an index finger at Terry. "You can't what-if yourself."

Seeing Terry's momentary frown, I added, "Second guess."

Morehouse showed his crabby side as he glanced at me. "He got it."

Terry looked at me. "But thanks, anyway."

Scoobie grinned broadly, then looked at Morehouse. "Any other things you want to tell Terry?"

Morehouse held up the card again. "The other medicines were for blood pressure and depression..."

"I think you meant his PTSD pills."

Scoobie had been sitting with one foot across the other knee, and his leg went to the floor. All three of us looked at him. I thought about how, at the funeral home the day after Terence died, Terry had said he "didn't know everything." He hadn't mentioned this. Had he seen it as a secret to keep, or something to keep to himself until he knew us better?

Scoobie flushed. "I didn't know he took medicine for that."

Terry tilted his head at Scoobie. "I think even before he met my mom. He said it helped him quit drinking too much." Terry grinned. "Except he said kick the sauce."

The things this child has had to understand.

Scoobie's jaw clenched for a moment and he nodded at Morehouse. "Anything else?"

Morehouse quit staring at Scoobie and looked back to Terry. "And he had some medicine for pain."

"Yep. From the cancer. It mostly worked."

Morehouse nodded. "Sometimes guys his age took more heart medicine, or maybe thyroid pills."

Terry shook his head. "Dad always said he had a good ticker."

Morehouse smiled. "Good to hear."

I thought his look at me could be called meaningful. Seemed the digitalis was not a usual medicine.

Morehouse stood. "Terry, you've been a big help."

"I have?"

"Yep. When someone doesn't have a list of medicines with them, and they pass, we just like to know what pills they took."

Terry shrugged. "I guess."

Morehouse stood and mussed Terry's hair the way I imagined he might do with his nephews. "You take care of Jolie and Scoobie, you hear?"

Terry smiled and Scoobie escorted Morehouse the short distance to the front door. Behind Morehouse's back, Terry looked at me, rolled his eyes, and ran his fingers through his hair.

Scoobie shut the door and faced us. "So, should we put your stuff in the chest?"

"Yeah, but well, I have a question. I guess for both of you."

I had not stood, and Terry sat back down next to me. Scoobie took the rocker and looked at me. I did the slightest of shrugs to let him know I had no clue.

Though he said he wanted to talk to both of us, Terry's eyes met Scoobie's. "You didn't know Dad had cancer, did you?"

"Here's the thing." Scoobie paused for several seconds as he studied his hands, which rested on his knees. He raised his head. "Your Dad, our Dad, wanted to talk to me a lot more, but the wedding...It seemed better that we talk after. I wish we had talked more."

Scoobie hadn't lied, but he had clearly sidestepped the truth. Plus, the only reason it seemed "better after the wedding" was because of Terry.

Terry's brows knitted. "But you didn't even know he was going to die."

"No." Scoobie straightened. "And the good news is that you're here."

Terry looked at Scoobie directly. "There's just one thing."

Scoobie nodded.

"When Dad and me didn't make it to the wedding, why didn't you look for us?"

Uh-oh.

Scoobie sat back in the rocker. "If you were older I'd tell you that's the $64,000 question."

"Huh?"

"From an old TV game show." Scoobie spread his hands. "Dad and I hadn't had a chance, hadn't talked in years."

Terry's eyes started to brim, and he straightened his shoulders. He seemed to be willing himself not to cry. "But, why not?"

Scoobie sighed. "You know how nice your mom was?"

We don't, but let's assume she was since Terry's such a good kid.

"Yeah." He stopped, I thought so he didn't cry.

"Well, my mother was not like that. Not one bit. I think when Terence cut ties with her he didn't want to…look back."

Terry sat very still. He finally leaned all the way back in the couch. His legs stuck out in front of him. "So you didn't even *know* about me?"

For the first time, Scoobie had a genuine smile. "I wish I had."

"But Dad, he talked about you all the time. I mean, not always, but, I dunno, lately."

I felt like a fifth wheel, and wished I weren't in the room. Not because I didn't care, but because this seemed very much a brother-to-brother conversation.

Scoobie waited a few seconds before speaking. "I think, maybe, he didn't know how to strike up contact again."

Terry's became insistent. "But he knew where you were!"

Scoobie's tone was gentle. "But he didn't know if I would want to see him."

Terry's voice was like a gunshot. "Did you?"

"I would have wanted to know the man Dad became after, after you were born. Maybe after he met your mom."

The seconds dragged by. I wanted to hug Terry, to tell him we were glad he came to us, but I could almost hear his brain processing.

Finally, he spoke. "Did you know him when he had the PTSD?"

"I believe I did. Plus...my mother might have made it worse."

Terry frowned. "What was her name?"

Scoobie almost snorted. "She used several, but she usually kept her first name as Penny."

Terry turned to look at me. "Did you know her?"

"I met her briefly, not long before she died." *Why did I say that? He'll ask how she died!*

"Did you like her?"

"Not one tiny bit."

Terry's eyebrows went up.

"And neither did Aunt Madge. She knew her longer."

"Huh." Terry looked at his knees and back at Scoobie. "Well, I'm sorry you had a mean mom. But I still don't understand."

Scoobie rubbed the back of his neck for a moment. "I think there are some things we may never understand." When Terry started to say something, he held up a palm toward him. "For now, I think we need to focus on the fact that he wanted us to know each other. He brought you to me because he knew he couldn't always be there."

Terry looked at me. "Did you send us a wedding invitation? I never saw one."

I smiled. "No. But I'm glad your dad found out about the wedding."

"How did he find out?"

Scoobie stood. "Now that really is the $64,000 question." He looked down at Terry. "I'll never tell you not to ask questions, but tomorrow is your first day in a new school. Plus, I have to go to work, and I'm wiped."

Terry stared at him for a moment, and apparently realized he wouldn't get answers to any more weighty questions tonight. "So, if you have to work, who's taking me to school? Aunt Madge?"

Scoobie grinned and nodded at me. "The pregnant woman."

CHAPTER TWENTY-TWO

I GLANCED AT TERRY as he sat next to me in the front seat. "My first day in school here wasn't 'til I was sixteen."

Terry gave me a sideways look as we pulled into the middle school parking lot. "Did your parents teach you at home?"

"Except for junior year, I lived in Lakewood, which is west of here. Long story. I'll tell you later."

"That's kind of like a bad movie preview."

I laughed out loud. "That's me, bad preview." I smiled at him as I put the car in park. "My basic point was that Scoobie was my first friend here. And look how that turned out."

"Kind of slowpokes."

We got out of the car and he slung the new backpack over his shoulders.

"Yep. We're kind of like the story of the tortoise and the hare."

He stared at the building entrance. "You and Scoobie know a lot of old-fashioned stuff."

"Be glad Aunt Madge or Harry didn't bring you."

He grinned. "She said I can visit after school and walk the dogs."

I nodded. "She'll want to hear all about your day." I did, too, but I planned to listen to her ask most of the questions, so I could get the hang of it.

SAM JEFFERSON HAD BEEN Terence's lawyer long ago. I was almost late for my nine-thirty appointment because I hadn't realized how many school forms I'd have to fill out. Or that after a teacher guided Terry to his classroom I'd be grilled on what kind of legal papers Scoobie and I had to prove we were his "guardians of record." Now I'd have two sets of questions for Jefferson.

His secretary led me into an immaculate office. Either all his records were digitized, or he had a great hiding place for the paper I usually associated with a law office.

Jefferson stood to extend a hand across a desk that was really more of a Queen Anne style table. I took in his white hair and trim build. He looked about sixty, but in our prior meeting I had not paid attention to his age. With his unlined, caramel skin he could have been closer to seventy.

"Good to see you, Jolie. Should I say Mrs. O'Brien?"

I sat in the proffered high-backed leather chair. "Socially, and as our baby's mom. I'm legally staying Jolie Gentil."

Jefferson nodded as he sat. "My daughters both kept our family name."

"Thank you for seeing me."

He nodded. "Not an easy situation to forget. Sad, in many ways."

"I have a couple of questions about establishing our custody for Terry, but mostly we'd like to know more about what you did for Mr. O'Brien."

"Sure. Since Scoobie is the child's adult brother, you should have no problem. I take it Terence left no paperwork for you?"

"Not that we've found. I suppose there could be something with an attorney in Florida."

"You can certainly wait until after the funeral to research it. No one in this town will question your role in the short term. Come back to me if you don't find anything."

My shoulders relaxed. "Good advice. Now, about what you did for Scoobie's father."

"Much of it is a matter of public record, though you'd have to go beyond digital records for it. I assume your husband is okay with me talking to you?"

I nodded. In fact, while I had told Scoobie I wanted to talk to his father's former lawyer, I hadn't let him know that I wanted most to know about the canceled request for a restraining order against Scoobie's mom. Surely it related to Terence's decision to leave. Maybe Sam Jefferson knew why Terence left alone.

"Scoobie's fine with it. He's working, and he's not sure he wants to know everything there is to know. He's kind of using me for a filter."

Jefferson nodded slowly.

"Oh, we'll pay you, of course."

He chuckled. "As I tell most clients, discussion of parameters is free for a few minutes. Seriously, if we end up pulling files or something that takes a while, we can talk about a bill."

"Great. I first noticed your name with Terence's alcohol-related arrests, but we're more interested in the divorce information, and any discussions of custody."

He grew somber. 'I knew Terence beyond serving as his attorney, of course."

When I looked surprised, he said, "VFW. We didn't serve in the same unit in Vietnam, but we were among the few Vietnam vets in town. Most young men who lived here could afford college and had deferments."

I sensed bitterness, but he smiled and gestured broadly, encompassing his office. "But, I got to come back, and without the G.I. bill, I wouldn't be here today."

"But Terence didn't use it?"

"Terence served in the infantry and had a much harder war. I was in the Signal Corps. When we laid cable, sometimes we got shot at. But it didn't compare to slogging through those rice patties in near-monsoon rains." He sighed. "And I never saw any of my friends blown to bits or run through with a knife."

I made it to his wastebasket in time, but it was only dry heaves. My sounds brought Sam Jefferson's secretary with a wad of tissues.

I stood. If brown skin can look pale, Jefferson's did. "I'm so sorry. I should have eaten a couple more crackers."

Seeing that I had not deposited anything in the basket, the secretary smiled. "I'm Lisa. I'll get you some ginger ale."

I moved toward my chair.

Jefferson approached his gingerly. "I should not have been so graphic."

I breathed slowly. "Truly, it's all me." I dabbed at my watering eyes and smiled. "I'm uh, glad you got to lay cable." I wanted to get back to Terence. "Did you know Terence before you went to Vietnam?"

He sat. "Just high school, and not well. The schools in Ocean Alley weren't segregated in the mid-1960s, but," he shrugged, "any interaction beyond classes was largely on sports teams."

"Ah. So, he came to you because of the VFW connection?"

"Yes. His wife, did you ever meet Penny?"

"Only briefly, before she died."

He shook his head. "Mean. I never expected her to come back to Ocean Alley. Not surprised she met her Maker here."

I nodded, wanting him to continue.

"Terence had messed up with the alcohol arrests, and she lorded that over him. He came to me because he wanted to leave her. Leave her and get custody of his son."

"I don't think Scoobie knows that last part."

"He took that kid a lot of places with him. When he was sober." He sighed and shook his head. "Penny hung out in the bars a lot, too. Now we would call children's services to check on a kid like Scoobie."

I suddenly remembered something Aunt Madge had said a couple of years ago. "I think maybe Aunt Madge did once."

Jefferson nodded. "It's hard to prove abuse, even neglect, unless there are obvious outward signs. I think we also pay more attention today."

I nodded. 'So, his dad tried for custody, you said?"

"Had me draw up a separation agreement that called for joint custody, but him to have sole physical custody."

"So what happened?"

"To use a military reference, she went ballistic."

"I can't believe she wanted Scoobie that badly."

"She didn't. But without him, she wouldn't get any child support."

My face must have shown confusion, because he added, "Terence had a partial disability. For his PTSD. He had a pension. Not big, but regular income."

To keep from heading for the wastebasket again, I stood to move to the window.

Jefferson waited for me to take some deep breaths. "You okay?"

"Yes, and I'm sorry to be so…distracting."

He smiled as the door opened and Lisa came in carrying a bottle of ginger ale and a glass of ice. "Sorry it took so long."

I returned to my chair. "Very gracious of you." She turned to leave and I began to pour. After a few small sips, I smiled at Jefferson "Nectar of the gods when you're pregnant."

"And I gather some of this is upsetting."

After a moment to collect my thoughts, I said, "If she actually received some form of child support, I don't think Scoobie ever knew that. He didn't even know if his father was alive."

"Payments would probably have stopped at eighteen, but I drew up the final papers for it to continue until that time. The money would have been automatically deducted from Terence's disability pension checks."

"So why didn't he come back? Why didn't he keep in touch?"

His tone softened. "To put it briefly, Terence was a mess. I'm no doctor, but I'd say he had severe PTSD. He drank to self-medicate." He shrugged. "Maybe he thought Scoobie would be better off without him."

"From what Scoobie's said, his mother made it sound that way," I murmured.

When I said nothing more, Jefferson said, "I'd be happy to talk to Scoobie, of course."

"I'll let him know. Can you think of anything else that's relevant to Terence, or Scoobie?"

He shook his head. "I would have been willing to stay in touch, but Terence never contacted me. He left...abruptly."

SAM JEFFERSON HAD THEN GIVEN me some general advice about proving our right to raise Terry. He thought Marti's military career meant Terence could have had some advice on instructions required to put Terry in the right hands, as Jefferson put it.

I mulled over everything Jefferson said as I stood in Harry's office going through the folders for recently completed appraisals. Since Steele Appraisals is just he and I, he had done the last four alone while I handled wedding details. Thankfully, business during the holidays had been light.

Equally thankfully, it had picked up now that we were in the new year. Two new requests were from banks that Lester Argrow worked with a lot. If a local bank underwrote the loan, it often worked pretty closely with the real estate agent.

Lester's recommendations have made him our biggest customer. He used to regularly argue with Harry when we said a house was worth less than a sales contract he had written, but he's calmed down. Ramona told me that a firm in Lakewood did a couple of appraisals for houses he had sales contracts for, and they came in way lower than anticipated.

The top folder of new requests had a handwritten note clipped to the file, in Lester's distinctive hand. "See if you can do better than the Jennifer dame."

Harry looked up from the computer and saw my smile. "You want to tell Jennifer Stenner he called her a dame, or you want me to?"

"She knows. At a Lions Club breakfast she told me she's thinking of charging him ten percent more for the insults."

Jennifer inherited Ocean Alley's larger appraisal firm from her father. Her grandfather began the firm, but she doesn't slide by because it's a family business. She is also very precise and dresses like a third-generation lawyer. She was kind of snobby when we went to high school together, but she's grown on me.

Harry chuckled. "You might want to head over to the house in the popsicle district today. I think it's supposed to snow again tomorrow."

The popsicle district is a section of Ocean Alley with mostly smaller bungalows. About ten years ago, a couple of neighbors painted their houses outlandishly bright colors, and most exterior paint jobs since then have followed suit.

I studied the file. "Gee, I wish this one had been on the market for us to look at. Three bedrooms, two baths, and a fenced back yard."

Harry stopped typing. "You're still going to look then?"

I nodded. "We've been saving. And, uh, Lester said Terry might be entitled to some income from Social Security or something. We could save some for him and justify using some for another bedroom."

"Hmm. You should probably check on his rights as the surviving child of someone in the military, too."

"This is getting complicated."

"Better to have greenbacks than not."

I agreed and headed to the house on Sea View Street. Since it was vacant, Lester had dropped off a key with Harry, and I didn't need to call ahead.

I pulled up in front of the royal blue house with bright white trim and shutters. It's harder to assess the exterior of a house when the ground is covered in snow. Appraisers aren't home inspectors, but we pay attention to things like cracks in the foundation. At least someone, probably Lester, had cleared the sidewalks from the weekend snow.

The front door had a deadbolt that required some wrestling, but eventually I figured that when I pulled the door toward me it unlocked. I breathed the warmer air deeply as I shut the door. The sellers must have planned on a quick settlement because they had left the heat on.

As I measured and took photos of the empty rooms, I couldn't help but envision the house with our furniture. The larger bedroom would be ours of course. The choice would be whether Terry or the baby got the mid-sized room. I needed to think about that before we had to confront such decisions.

Babies had a lot of paraphernalia and I'd need a rocker to sit in to feed him or her. I hoped Terry would see it that way. Of course, pre-teen boys could accumulate sports equipment, and Terry would need a desk and room for books. Maybe we'd need a bigger house than I thought.

CHAPTER
TWENTY-THREE

I FINISHED WITH THE bungalow and wrote up the appraisal at the office by one o'clock. I told Terry I would pick him up at school at two-thirty. We would stop by Aunt Madge's for a snack before heading home to get the house ready for a visit from Frank and Linda Booker.

In the meantime, I would swing by the hospital to talk to the medical examiner about TAT. *Oops. Terence.*

Sunday night, Morehouse had left us a summary statement from Dr. O'Malley's report. Cancer and organ failure were primary causes of death, with a reference to cardiac arrhythmia. But the report raised the possibility of unexpected medication interaction. Apparently she had decided not to denote the death as suspicious, but wanted to leave the option open as to where the medications came from.

At the hospital, I cheated and parked in the ER parking lot, which was closer to an entrance and the elevator. I didn't want to run into a lot of people who would ask about that morning's obituary, which named Scoobie and Terry as survivors, or the next day's funeral service. Wedding congratulations I wouldn't mind, but I figured death would interest more people.

The tread on my boots squelched on the tile floor and water from slushy snow puddled around my feet in the elevator. As the elevator opened on the basement, home to the morgue and medical examiner's office, I almost ran head-on into Elmira Washington. Technically, she nearly ran into me as she barreled into the elevator, head down.

I sidestepped her so as not to be knocked into the back of the car. "Elmira!"

She stood back and peered up at me from her height of five-one. "Jolie. Just who I wanted to see."

Nuts.

"I'm getting off here, Elmira."

She backed out and stood on the tile floor as I joined her. Her wool coat had a couple more food stains, and her steel-gray hair, though short, was mussed. "Me, too, then."

"What can I do for you?" *Besides plot my escape.*

"That man who died was Scoobie's father."

I nodded. "We're aware of it."

"I saw him in Newhart's the other night, when you and Scoobie talked to me. But you weren't sitting with him."

I let a couple of seconds pass before saying, "I know."

"George talked to me about him. I knew Terence O'Brien."

"Well?"

She shook her head. "He was Catholic and I'm not, so I didn't know him well."

If they'd known each other as children in probably the 1950s, they likely traveled in different circles. Still, it was an odd distinction to make in the 21st century. "You must have run into each other around town."

"Oh yes. But he left many years ago."

"You are welcome to join us tomorrow for the funeral." *Not really, but it's open to anyone.* "We're holding it at Peters Funeral Home."

"I want to know how he died."

If I said "none of your business" she'd make it sound as if I had been deliberately rude to her. I didn't need that. "He had cancer. You probably saw that in the paper."

She waved a hand under my nose, clearly dismissing an illness as cause of death. "They don't keep bodies in the hospital for days when it's natural causes."

God help me. "Sometimes on holiday weekends things take longer."

She studied me, her narrow eyes becoming slits. "I don't think holidays had anything to do with it. He was kind of a lush when he lived here. Maybe his liver gave out."

I could almost feel my gaze steel, and she backed away a step. "Elmira, we are talking about my husband's father. What you think…is not relevant." I pushed past her.

I headed toward the ME's office. To my back, she said, "I'm just trying to help."

That did it. Almost three years of having Elmira Washington gossip about me or whoever crossed her path came to a head. I turned abruptly to face her. "No, you're snooping. You love to be in the know, especially if what you learn is private business. Then you walk around town as if, as if…"

Elmira's face reddened and her expression contorted.

Telling her what I thought of her had not been rewarding after all. I swallowed. "I'm sorry, Elmira. That was rude."

An orderly turned the corner and came toward us pushing a cart piled high with pink plastic drinking pitchers and yellow plastic bedpans. I felt a strong need to say something about working a problem from both ends. Instead, I looked back to Elmira.

She whispered. "If I don't have news, no one will want to talk to me."

I fished a tissue from the pocket of my parka and handed it to her. "You might find out more people will talk to you if they don't have to watch what they say."

She blew her nose.

The orderly stopped next to us and pushed the elevator button. He looked to be about thirty-five and had the kind of paunch acquired when someone drinks a lot of beer and forgets they should eat less to counter the added calories.

"You ladies need any help?"

Elmira started to say something, but I said, "No."

The elevator dinged and he stepped on, the door shutting behind him.

I looked down at Elmira. "You can come to Terence's funeral tomorrow. Remember what I said. If you don't gossip and pry, you may find more people want to talk to you." I walked quickly toward the ME's office.

Elmira did not follow me. Small favors.

I pushed through the glass door and stood in the stark outer office of the woman who thought it possible that Terence O'Brien's death could have been hastened by cardiac arrhythmia brought on by digitalis, a medicine it did not appear that Scoobie's dad took.

The sliding glass counter door that separated patients and family from the medical staff had a small round lock. I noted a sign that said "ring for service" and put my palm on the top of an enclosed, round bell.

Light steps came from around the corner and Dr. O'Malley walked toward me. "Jolie." She peered behind me. "No Scoobie?"

"He's working." I pulled her report from my purse and raised it to her line of vision. "Sergeant Morehouse dropped off a copy of your summary report. It would be a bit easier for Scoobie if I talked to you. He might follow up, but he probably won't have to."

She hesitated only briefly. Since she knows Scoobie, me and, more important, Aunt Madge, I figured she would discuss Terence with me. *Thanks goodness for small towns.*

"Sure, come on back to my office. You probably already know that the funeral home picked up Mr. O'Brien."

I didn't, but I sure as heck had not planned on seeing him. "Fine by me." I realized I'd sounded cavalier. "I just meant I don't think I've ever been in a hospital morgue when I knew someone, um, in residence."

She gestured to a chair across from her desk, and I sat. From her quick glance at the clock, I knew she had little time to spare.

She tapped a pen on her desk. "Let's get right to it. You're aware that I've indicated digitalis may have played a role in his death. Initially, I didn't see any problems. He had advanced cancer and really banged his head and face on the steering wheel when he hit that pole."

"So, you were primarily looking for why he passed out, or whatever?"

She nodded. "I couldn't easily see why. In terms of his heart, which is what the digitalis acts on, the first couple EKGs done in the ER showed abnormal T waves. That can be an indication of myocardial disease, possibly infarction, or heart attack as we call it. Abnormal T waves can indicate a digitalis overdose, but we had no reason to suspect that for Mr. O'Brien."

"In some circumstances, I don't mind issuing a death certificate that says something like 'immediate cause of death undetermined,' and lists complications of other illnesses."

"But you didn't want to do that?" I asked.

"If he had arrived at the hospital after death, I might have had to be satisfied with that. However, since he was alive, we did blood work over several hours. Here again, if he had a prescription for the drug, an accidental overdose would have been a natural supposition. Heck, at his age and state of health, it wouldn't have taken an overdose, just an unfortunate interaction."

"But he didn't have a prescription?"

"Nowhere in the VA system. If he had stopped at a clinic of some type on the drive up here, maybe he would have gotten a prescription. Though I doubt an urgent care doc would have prescribed that particular medicine and sent him on his way." She pointed a pen at me. "But the little boy, Scoobie's brother, right? He didn't mention his dad feeling ill on the trip."

"No. Scoobie told me the drug can lead to arrhythmia. Is that what happened?"

"I think it very possible. If he had been healthy otherwise, and conscious, the hospital could have done more to counter the irregular heartbeat. Without any medical history, it's harder to treat someone who can't communicate."

"And because you found digitalis in his system, you're pretty sure that's what killed him?"

"Hard to be sure of much. What we have is an anomaly, and no reason to expect one."

"We, uh, haven't actually seen the death certificate."

"The funeral home should have been able to get the certified copy from the Department of Public Health today. You saw from the summary report that I indicated the advanced nature of his cancer and early stage of kidney failure as primary causes. Potential medication interaction resulting in cardiac arrhythmia was noted as a possible contributing factor."

"But you don't mention digitalis poisoning?"

"Not for me to say. Up to the police to decide if it's something they want to pursue. Maybe he had a long-ago prescription for the drug – though I find no indication – maybe a couple years ago some good buddy gave him some. Who knows? It mostly matters –- to me and people like you -- if someone gave it to him without his knowledge or consent."

She glanced at the clock again.

Though I had a better understanding of the factors that contributed to Terence O'Brien's death, I didn't feel like I had solid answers. But I had all Dr. O'Malley could provide. I stood. "I've taken a lot of your time. I don't know where all this will end up, but it will help Scoobie a lot to have more information."

She stood, reached across the desk, and shook my hand. "How is the little boy?"

Though she didn't ask, I sensed she wondered how big a surprise Terence and Terry had been to us. Given that Scoobie and I – and Aunt Madge and Harry – are friendly with a lot of people, she probably figured knowledge of Scoobie's dad and a seemingly recently found little brother would have preceded their arrival.

"He'll be okay. We're just really glad they made it to Ocean Alley before Mr. O'Brien died."

She nodded, somberly. "Thank God they weren't on an interstate when he passed out."

RAMONA SAID THE SAME THING when I stopped at the Purple Cow Office Supply before picking up Terry at school.

"I liked the obituary. I didn't know his dad served in Vietnam." Her statement was more of a question. Ramona loves to be in the know. While her job at the Purple Cow makes her a local purveyor of news for many, she doesn't have the gossipy edge that Elmira does.

"Scoobie has some memory of going to the VFW with his father, but he doesn't remember any details."

She tilted her head, kind of studying me before deciding to speak. "I barely knew Scoobie in elementary school. Jennifer Stenner said his dad would walk him to school sometimes. She said a couple kids made fun of Scoobie because they held hands occasionally."

I stared at her, then shook my head. "I don't think he remembers...." I let my voice trail off. "He might like to know that, but maybe not immediately."

Her eyebrows went up. "He doesn't remember?"

If it had been someone else, I wouldn't have replied. I chose my words carefully. "I don't think he's even sure what he remembers, but...it might be better to let him come to terms with that himself."

Ramona picked up a couple of pens from the glass counter and added them to a pencil box next to the cash register. "I'm just listening, not repeating."

I could tell I hurt her feelings, and felt bad. "I'm not saying you would pass that around. I just honestly think he has a lot of processing to do before he thinks about what to say."

She nodded stiffly, and long strands of her blonde hair fell from a crocheted wrap that covered the bun set atop her head. "Terry okay?"

I smiled. "You know, if someone had said a ten-year old we never knew about came into our wedding and lit up our lives, I'd have told them it was impossible. And yet, here we are."

I FELT LESS OPTIMISTIC after being greeted by a very quiet Terry at the end of the school day. I'm not sure what I expected, but since he'd been so excited to get to school, somber wasn't it.

"Did you like your teachers?"

"They're okay."

"Uh, did you see Kevin, the sergeant's nephew?"

"In the cafeteria."

"Anything you want to talk about?"

"They had math and history books for me, but they have to find an extra book for English."

I had no clue how to proceed, but fortunately we were close to the Cozy Corner. "Aunt Madge always has cheddar cheese bread for guests in the afternoon, but since she doesn't have any guests right now, I heard a rumor about cinnamon buns."

He grinned. "We can always count on Aunt Madge."

If I didn't think so too, I would have been insulted.

He said nothing else, but greeted the dogs enthusiastically.

"Young man, how about a piece of fresh bread before that cinnamon bun?" Aunt Madge asked. She had several pieces of bread on a serving dish, and Terry selected a small one. Probably leaving room for the bun.

Perhaps sensing his quiet mood suggested a stressful day, after Terry had eaten a few mouthfuls, Aunt Madge said, "First days at new schools can have a lot of challenges."

He shrugged. "The teachers were nice. And that guy Kevin, Sergeant Morehouse's nephew, talked to me. But he's a grade ahead."

"Did you meet some nice kids in your grade?" I asked.

He shrugged again and looked at Aunt Madge. "Do you get the paper?"

If the question surprised her, she didn't show it. "I do. Do you need an extra copy of your dad's obituary?"

I could have smacked myself. We'd been so rushed, I hadn't opened the paper before Terry left for school.

"Yeah. When the homeroom teacher introduced me, she said I wouldn't be there tomorrow because of Dad's funeral. A couple kids knew. From the paper. I mean, they didn't know I'd be there, their parents knew Scoobie and saw my name with his."

Aunt Madge stayed focused on Terry. "Some families read the newspaper at the breakfast table."

Terry turned to me. "That might be a good idea."

CHAPTER
TWENTY-FOUR

TERRY WAS SO EXCITED about Frank and Linda Booker's Monday evening arrival that he cheerfully used a spray bottle to clean every window in the living room.

When Scoobie hadn't gotten home by four-thirty, I began to wonder if I had forgotten that he had some appointment. Ten minutes later, a horn honked in front of our house.

Terry, probably hoping it was the Bookers, ran to the window. "Hey, that's Dad's car. We've been so busy I forgot all about it."

So busy. I guess that was one way of looking at our revised lives. I opened the front door. "I forgot about it, too. Sergeant Morehouse said they had taken it to the police station, and we needed to pick it up."

Terry stood next to me. "Do we need three cars?"

"I don't think so. We can talk about it in a day or so."

A moment later a car pulled up behind Scoobie. I looked more closely. "Ah. George drove Scoobie's car back. Probably Scoobie will have to take George wherever his car is."

Scoobie waved to us and pointed to his car. I looked down at Terry. "I think he's saying he's driving George now."

"Can I go with them?"

"Not sure." I opened the door to a blast of cold air, and leaned out. "Scoobie. OK to have company on the drive to George's?"

"If he's ready now," Scoobie called.

Terry dashed to a peg on the wall to grab his coat and was out the door in five seconds. "See you soon!"

I watched him greet Scoobie and George and climb into the back seat of Scoobie's car. He's so comfortable so fast, I thought.

As I shut the door, Pebbles waddled into the living room.

"You need to get used to Terry. He's going to live here."

Pebbles ignored me and moseyed toward either her food bowl in the kitchen or her litter box in the closet by the back door. Jazz rose from a spot in front of the living room heating vent and followed her.

"Okay, you're both hungry." I filled their food bowls and wiped the kitchen counters one more time. I felt self-conscious about having two strangers in the house. I liked our little bungalow, but no one could call it elegant.

"Who cares?" I decided to sit for a few minutes while I had a chance. I pulled out my to-do list for tomorrow's funeral and found we had completed everything.

I had a separate list that dealt with things like looking for a will or figuring out if we had to go through probate for Terence O'Brien. However, I decided to take Sam Jefferson's advice to deal with that after the funeral.

I leaned back in the rocker and tried to imagine what Frank and Linda Booker would look like. "Hmm. They're from Florida. Probably blonde and tanned."

THOUGH IT WAS ONLY FIVE-THIRTY when the Bookers arrived, it was dark and cold. They had texted us when they got close, so Terry had his nose pressed to the front window when they arrived. "They're here! They're here!"

Before I could tell him to put on his coat, he shot out the door. The steps were shoveled and dry, but he almost slid across a small patch of snow near the driveway.

Frank stepped out of their dark blue Toyota first and grabbed Terry in a bear hug. Linda ran around the car from the passenger side and joined the two for a three-way embrace.

My estimate of their looks was off. Linda had long brown hair that was pulled back in a French braid. Frank had broad shoulders and, from what I could see from our doorway, dark brown or black hair.

Scoobie tapped me lightly on the back of the head. "Good scene for a movie."

I nodded. "He said he missed them a lot."

The threesome walked up the porch together and Scoobie and I ushered them into the house. Frank Booker had a firm handshake and a warm smile. Linda's bright eyes roamed our living room and came to rest on me. "It's good to meet you. Did Terry bring his coat?"

Before I could respond, Terry said, "I have it. I didn't need it to run out for a minute."

He appeared used to Linda giving instructions, but I felt as if she was implying that I should take better care of him. I pushed the thought aside. I was probably just nervous.

As Scoobie shut the door, he said, "Maybe before we settle in here for supper we should lead the Bookers to the Cozy Corner to give them a chance to freshen up after their long drive."

I smiled. "Good idea. You'll have a lot more room to change clothes over there."

I'd already talked to Aunt Madge about wanting the Bookers to eat at our place. I thought it would seem more like Terry welcoming them to his new home. Plus, I wanted to establish that Scoobie and I were now his…well, not parents, but sort of.

"ARE YOU SURE YOU wouldn't like to eat here?" Harry asked, as we prepared to leave.

I shook my head. "We won't be fancy, but Arnie agreed to do a carryout of his crab and cheese casserole for us. It's already in our fridge." I smiled at Linda. "Then you'll really know you're in New Jersey."

Linda had changed from the jeans and sweatshirt she'd worn on the road to a pair of hunter green casual slacks and a bright yellow sweater with a dolphin insignia. She pointed to the dolphin and grinned at Terry. "Crabs for New Jersey. Dolphins for Florida."

He smiled at her and then Scoobie. "Frank and Linda took me to Sea World the week after Mom died. I loved the dolphins."

"Lucky you," Aunt Madge said, as Scoobie, Harry, and I nodded agreement. She handed me a plastic bag with a sliced loaf of fresh bread. "Add this to your menu."

Terry beamed. "I made bread Friday. Well," he looked to Aunt Madge, "I mean, I had help."

Scoobie took Terry's coat off the back of a chair and held it for him. "You can lecture us on your bread-making skills while we eat at home."

WE ATE A PLEASANT DINNER, but I still had a hard time feeling at ease. I finally decided it was because Linda Booker was trying so hard to make it clear that she had a special bond with Terry. Or maybe I was imagining it.

I told myself to quit being a bitch.

After dinner, Linda surprised Terry by pulling from her small tote the ingredients for his favorite cookies. "Unless I need to buy eggs?" she asked me. "I figured you had them."

"We do indeed." I started for the fridge.

Linda gave me a brilliant smile. "I can help myself."

Yes you do. OK. Now I really am a bitch.

Frank grinned at Scoobie and me. "I don't know about you, but I'm out of the kitchen until I smell baking cookies."

I found Frank easy to be around. As we settled ourselves in the living room, Scoobie spoke softly. "I'd like to duck out for a few minutes. I told Father Teehan I'd drop off a copy of the prayers Terry and I picked, and I simply haven't gotten around to it."

"Sure," I said, and Frank nodded.

Scoobie glanced toward the kitchen and then at Frank. "Don't want you to think I'm a fibber, but I'm going to tell my little 'bro I'm heading out to pick up snack foods for tomorrow."

"That's probably a good idea anyway," I said. "People might hang out here, you know, after."

Scoobie stuck his head in the kitchen to announce his shopping trip, and got little reaction. Terry concentrated on the cookies.

When he left, Frank and I cocked our heads toward the kitchen, listening to Terry and Linda.

"So, Aunt Madge taught me how to bake bread. Are cookies harder or easier?"

"You have to measure carefully and all that, but you don't have to knead the cookie dough."

"Yeah," Terry said, "that was a lot of work."

Frank and I glanced at each other, and I smiled. "They really seem to like each other."

His eyes looked at the floor and back to me. "Terry likes me, but since his mom died, Linda's been his touchstone. He came to our place every day after school."

"Gosh. What a big…wait, Terence didn't work, did he?"

Frank shook his head. "He was finishing a round of chemo, so he didn't feel at all well the last few weeks. Linda made a big deal of Christmas, since we thought it was Terence's last one."

I took a breath so deep it came out like a sigh. "You don't have to answer this, but did you think you would have Terry after his dad died?"

Frank nodded. "Terence never actually said it. I don't think he really thought he'd die until the last couple of weeks. That's when he told Terry, and us, that he'd like to take a trip to Jersey, to show Terry where he lived before Florida."

"Ah. Did he, uh, mention Scoobie?"

"Not specifically. He told Linda and me that he had family he hadn't been in touch with for years." He paused, but continued. "That was the first time I sensed he might have other plans for Terry. We sat him down one night after Terry went to bed, and told him we'd be proud to raise Terry."

I whispered, "That was really good of you."

"It's not like we were making a sacrifice. He brought a lot of joy, especially after…"

He had paused, so I added, in a lower voice, "Terry mentioned Linda was pregnant at one point."

Frank nodded. "Boy, were we excited. But," he spread his hands, "the doctors said it's not uncommon for a woman to lose her first baby."

Breaking glass and an alarmed "uh oh" came from the kitchen. Terry's voice held distress. "Jolie, I…"

Linda laughed. "It's a juice glass, Terry. We can clean it up."

I didn't bother to stand. "No worries."

"No, Jazz!"

Terry's voice had been commanding, and Jazz streaked past, en route to the bedroom.

I smiled at Frank. "Must have been a glass of milk."

We listened for a moment as Linda cleaned up the glass – "so you don't get hurt" – and the pair went back to their recipe.

Frank nodded at my midriff. "Your first?"

"Yes, we call it our unexpected blessing. We're both thrilled."

"How did you guys meet?"

I briefly told the story of knowing each other for a year in high school and reconnecting just a few years ago. I left out any reference to Scoobie sometimes majoring in marijuana in college or my ex-husband's embezzlement tendencies.

"You guys were lucky, too," he said. "We were both married young and had been divorced for many years before we met each other. We were really excited."

I nodded, knowing he meant the baby. "I hope you can have a next time."

"We hope so, too." He cleared his throat and his voice rose to a traditional conversational level from the quiet tone of our discussion. "It's really great of you to welcome us like this. It's helped both of us to meet Terry's new family, especially Linda."

I wanted to take the conversation back to Terry's relationship with the Bookers. Given that they seemed so close, I didn't understand why Terence wanted to bring his younger son to Scoobie. "How did Terence react when you said you would love to raise Terry?"

He sighed. "It may have been too much, too soon. I'd spoken to a lawyer about the kind of instructions Terence would need to leave so that Terry came to us immediately. We didn't know about other family, and couldn't stand the idea of him being in foster care."

"Sounds smart."

"It may have been smart, but I think it spooked Terence. Made his death seem more likely or something. He realized he wanted to see his older son."

What he said made sense. "It may not have been a rejection of you, his bringing Terry here. Maybe he just wanted to...examine all his options."

Frank sighed. "We kind of think so, too. But we can see," he gestured in a semi-circle, "that Terry is thrilled to have found you guys. We think that Terry didn't know about you until just before they left."

I smiled. "We sensed that he'd had an idea of New Jersey family, but maybe not Scoobie. I doubt he could have kept that secret for long."

He frowned. "Terence only found out his...close timeline in the week before they left. We figured he told Terry about you guys in part so he'd know he wasn't alone."

I felt as if Frank had recognized Terry would stay with us. At the very least, I now knew they didn't have a statement from Terence that would establish them as the preferred people to raise his young son. I wondered if Linda would agree.

EXHAUSTION GRIPPED BOTH OF us as we climbed into bed. Even so, I sketched my conversations with Sam Jefferson and Frank.

Scoobie said nothing when I told him his father's lawyer mentioned Terence wanted to have custody of Scoobie. After several seconds with no comment, I relayed Frank Booker's offer to Terence to raise Terry.

Scoobie turned head on the pillow to face me. "Sounds as if they won't challenge us." He faced the ceiling again and blew out a breath. "I'm up to my eyeballs. Do you mind if we talk about all this more after the funeral?"

"Of course not." I propped on an elbow to lean over to kiss his cheek. "Like you say, it'll be there tomorrow."

Scoobie smiled. "Good to know you listen sometimes."

It seemed uncouth to give him the finger the night before his father's funeral.

Scoobie fell asleep almost instantly. I stared at the ceiling for several minutes. Knowing Terry had other options hadn't made either of us want him to return to Florida.

Plus, Aunt Madge would probably never forgive us. I could hear her say, "How could you let that child think he wasn't wanted? After all he's been through?"

We couldn't. Nor did we want to.

CHAPTER TWENTY-FIVE

TUESDAY MORNING, SCOOBIE SAID he needed to run an errand and would meet us at the funeral home. I had assumed we would go together, and hoped I would say the right thing if Terry asked any questions.

Terry watched the door shut behind Scoobie and then faced me. He looked so grown up in the navy blue blazer and blue plaid tie that Aunt Madge had bought him that I didn't expect the uncertainty in his voice. "Do you think we should ask Aunt Madge to drive us?"

I longed to call her, but this seemed a time to establish my worth as an adult in his life. "She and Harry wouldn't mind, and" – I mimicked a line from a popular movie – "Harry is an excellent driver. But I think we're good on our own for a few minutes."

He grinned. "You sound like your friend, George."

"Damn."

Terry laughed. "I like him."

"I usually do. You need to use the bathroom before we leave?"

He rolled his eyes. "I'm ten, not two."

Chalk that up to a question I don't need to ask in the future.

We stepped into the thirty-five-degree air and I breathed deeply. Last night's snow had been only a dusting, and would be gone as soon as the sun shone on the pavement for an hour. "It's January, but the weather seems more like spring is on the way."

"In Florida we call this an Arctic blast."

Humor must run in families.

"We do need to buy you a warmer jacket."

He spoke quickly. "I'm okay with what I have."

"I know, but…"

"Really, I don't need anything."

I pulled the key fob out of my pocket, but didn't open the driver's side door. "If you're worried about money, you don't have to."

"You guys aren't rich."

"We are not rich. But we have what we need. Plus," I debated saying anything more, but decided to forge ahead, "our friend Lester said you might be eligible for some Social Security payments or something. Because, you know, your parents died."

I pushed the button and the car's automatic locking system burped. I pressed the unlock button again for the passenger door. "Too cold to stand outside."

Terry opened the side door and slid in next to me. "Huh. That's good, I guess."

I started the car. "We have lots of stuff to find out, but the bottom line is it makes no difference whether you get any financial support. We are all glad you found us."

"You are?"

How does he not know this? I decided to try humor rather than more reassurance. "You are willing to learn to change diapers, aren't you?"

"The throwaway kind?"

"You are a hoot. Yes, disposable diapers."

He grinned. "Dad said if people were watching from outer space, they would never be able to figure out why we saved the other kind instead of throwing them away."

I had an even better idea of where Scoobie got his weird humor.

TERRY SAID NOTHING DURING the rest of the drive to the Peters Funeral Home. Since I still thought I gave lame answers to half of Terry's questions, I didn't mind the silence.

The funeral didn't start for forty-five minutes, so the only cars in the lot were Scoobie's, parked near the entrance, and staff cars in the back of the lot. Frank and Linda were going to drive over with Madge and Harry. She told me she suggested that to be sure they didn't get there too early. I thought Aunt Madge wanted to ensure our little nuclear family had time together.

We planned our early arrival to give us time to gather with other family members down the hall from the viewing room. However, Mr. Peters guided Terry and me into the chapel where TAT's service was to be held.

Scoobie stood at the front, near the closed coffin. Several floral displays and plants lined the wall on each side of the coffin. Not nearly as many as when our friend Lance Wilson died, but half of First Presbyterian Church had turned out for him.

Peters left us in the doorway, and Terry and I stood for a moment at the back of the room.

When I started to go toward Scoobie, Terry whispered, "Wait here a second." He straightened his shoulders and moved toward Scoobie, whose slight change in posture told me he was aware of our presence.

Terry hesitated momentarily, then stood next to Scoobie and took his hand.

Scoobie sniffed. "Hey, buddy."

"You want a Kleenex?"

"Sure." Scoobie took the slightly wrinkled one Terry pulled from his pocket. He first dabbed his eyes, then blew his nose.

"Are you going to miss Dad?"

Scoobie hesitated. "I wish I'd known him well enough to miss him more."

Terry looked up at him and back at the coffin, whose closed lid was at his eye level. "Me too. It would've meant I knew you. I coulda used a brother."

Scoobie grinned and looked down at him. "Me, too."

OUR FAMILY GATHERING ROOM held a diverse lot. Renée and Julia arrived soon after we did. Terry appeared delighted to see Julia and immediately took her to a small bulletin board that sat on an easel not far from the room entrance. Terry created it, and the board would be moved to the funeral home entry area in a few minutes.

Elaine L. Orr

Terry had a four-by-six photo album of snapshots of his Florida family, as he called his parents and the Bookers, and selected about ten photos for the board. Unknown to him, I had asked the funeral home to take them off the board last night and scan copies. I thought losing any of them would be close to catastrophic. The staff had replaced the photos nearly as Terry had them, and Terry made some adjustments as he explained them to a rapt Julia.

I could have hugged her twice.

George, as the closest person to a brother Scoobie had until Terry arrived, stood with Scoobie at a table that boasted iced tea and hot drinks. I sat with Ramona and Renée on an old-fashioned loveseat, careful not to spill my hot tea on the carved wood or rose-colored upholstery.

Renée nodded at my abdomen. "You taking care of yourself?"

"Yes. When I got tired last night I sat on the couch and closed my eyes for a few minutes."

She and Ramona said, "Good."

Ramona smoothed her black cotton skirt. "Did you like the couple that came up from Florida?"

"The Bookers care a lot about Terry," I said.

Ramona turned slightly to face me. "That's the answer to a different question."

I sat up straighter. "They are very likeable. I'm probably...uneasy because they would love to have become Terry's adoptive parents."

Renée spoke softly. "I wondered about that when they drove so far for such a short time."

"Terry seems happy," Ramona said. "I mean, besides losing his dad."

As if on cue, the hallway door opened and Linda Booker strode in, followed by Aunt Madge, with Harry and Frank Booker behind her. Linda's eyes locked on Terry and she walked briskly to him and gathered him for a hug.

When he stiffened rather than return the hug, she pulled back and her smile froze. Terry's did not. He smiled and politely gestured to Julia. "This is my new cousin, Julia. I met her after Scoobie's wedding."

Ramona grinned as she whispered, "Scoobie's wedding."

Renée smiled as she stood to go to Julia and Terry. "It's all in your perspective," she murmured. She extended her hand to the immaculately attired Linda. In a black suit with a bright white collar and black choker necklace, she could have been mistaken for the wife of the deceased at a wealthy real estate broker's funeral.

As Renée approached her, Linda waved briefly to me, and then turned so she could talk to Renée without looking in my direction. I stayed seated watching introductions, and smiled lightly at Frank as he nodded to me.

Harry helped himself to coffee as Aunt Madge took Renée's seat. "You look alive and well. Did you sleep?"

"I did. None of us woke up until seven. I would have gone longer, but Jazz wanted food."

Aunt Madge leaned forward so she could see across me to Ramona. "The silk flower display you brought is lovely."

I turned toward Ramona. "I didn't see them."

She flushed. "Thanks. I didn't finish until last night. And I think a bunch of flowers are arriving in the other room. People only saw the obituary yesterday, and of course hardly anyone knew Scoobie still had a living father."

"Lots of questions down at the Purple Cow?" I asked.

She shrugged. "Mostly people asking if Scoobie is okay. Everybody wants to know about Terry and whether Scoobie knew about him."

"How on earth do you answer that?" Aunt Madge asked.

I glanced at her with a smile. "Looking for tips?"

"Depending on who it is, I tell them Scoobie is delighted to have found a brother. Or mind their own beeswax," Aunt Madge said.

"I'd like to be a fly on the wall for some of the latter," I said.

Father Teehan and Reverend Jamison arrived together and went to Scoobie.

Aunt Madge stood. "I'm so glad they're both here." She left us for them.

I leaned back in the loveseat.

Ramona patted down the collar of the yellow shirt I wore under a blue sweater. "You, uh, going to just sit here?"

My eyes narrowed as I looked at Linda greeting Father Teehan like an old friend. "Partly I'm saving my energy, mostly I'm observing."

THE SERVICE ITSELF WAS much less stressful than I imagined. Had it only been five days ago that many people here had been in the Cozy Corner for our wedding?

But not all. The almost seventy-five attendees had gathered for Scoobie – a few people from the hospital and college, several from his high school graduating class, Elmira, of course, and a cross-section of his AA and Al-Anon buddies.

I got a kick out of hearing people ask, "How do you know Scoobie?" and hearing answers like, "Just from around town," or "Gee, it's been so long I don't remember."

A few people who knew Terence had come. Sam Jefferson introduced himself and several VFW colleagues to Terry before the formal service started. Terry seemed almost in awe of them.

George sidled up to me as I settled in the front row. "Nice to see a crowd."

I nodded agreement.

He leaned toward my ear. "You heard it's better to be seen than viewed?" He moved away before I could elbow him, but I saw Ramona get in a good nudge as they sat in the second row. Idly I wondered if they were dating. Maybe Michelle and Julia would get their wish.

Father Teehan and Reverend Jamison alternated the readings, which pleased Scoobie. He leaned toward me and whispered, "Was that your idea?"

I shook my head. We'd told Father Teehan to do his thing as he wanted. He had the lead because of Terry's preference, but Scoobie and I are "on the Protestant side of the aisle," as Scoobie had explained to Terry previously. That and the fact that Reverend Jamison hosts Harvest for All made him a welcome addition to the funeral team.

Near the end of the service, Terry stood to hand Father Teehan a wrinkled three-by-five card. Father examined it and smiled. "You want to read it?"

Terry shook his head.

Father Teehan smiled at the group. "Terry said his mother, Marti, often recited this verse from 1st Corinthians. She told him it was read when she married Terence."

Love is patient, love is kind. It does not envy, it does not boast, it is not proud. It does not dishonor others, it is not self-seeking, it is not easily angered, it keeps no record of wrongs. Love does not delight in evil but rejoices with the truth. It always protects, always trusts, always hopes, always perseveres."

Ramona cried and I stifled tears. I thought if I started I wouldn't be able to stop.

Because burial would take place later, we were having light snacks at the funeral home before dispersing. Or that's what I thought. But when Mr. Peters led us downstairs a feast lay before us.

Many of the Harvest for All volunteers and a few patrons stood behind the buffet ready to serve us. I blubbered my way through introductions as I explained the food pantry to Frank and Linda and the varied roles the different food servers played.

I almost totally lost it when we got to Max. I figured he'd avoided the funeral because he didn't like crowds, but he'd apparently been helping prepare food.

Linda took his hand. "Well, Mr. Max, Terry told me you were one of the first of Scoobie's friends that he met. At the library, wasn't it?"

Max beamed and I could have hugged her for knowing how to make him feel comfortable.

Frank Booker regaled Sam Jefferson and other VFW members with 'Terence stories,' as he called them. He said Terence, who took care of Terry while Marti worked, was a doting dad, but sometimes an embarrassing one.

Terry joined Frank in telling a story about a time Terence chaperoned a school trip to a communications exhibit and told a lecturer he thought smartphones made people stupid. Anytime the lecturer mentioned something the phone did, such as recite directions, Terence had an alternative. Such as maps. Finally the frustrated lecturer said they could be used to read books. Terence said he withdrew his point.

I sat a table away from the revelry, but anyone in the room could hear the stories and ensuing guffaws. Scoobie stopped talking to Harry as they stood near the buffet table, and his eyes met mine. His expression was easily readable, at least to me. "Why couldn't my life have been like that?"

As one who had dealt with his own addiction to alcohol and a pot predilection, Scoobie understood changed behavior, at least at an intellectual level. I sighed to myself. All of this would take a long time to work through.

As people drifted away, I headed to where Linda stood talking to Megan. I intended to ask if I could help with cleanup.

"So Linda," Megan said, "do you work on the Air Force Base?"

Linda shook her head. "I'm a home health aide. In fact, I was able to be assigned to help take care of Marti her last couple months. She didn't want to go to a hospice facility until the last week or so."

Okay, I was glad a friend could help her, and probably Terry, but it further stressed how close she had been to Terry. No wonder she thought she should be raising him. Cherishing him, really.

I walked next to the two. "I didn't know that, Linda. How fortunate for them."

Less animated than when she'd talked to Megan, she nodded. "For all of us."

"You need help putting things away, Megan?"

"As if. I'm in no rush. I closed Java Jolt and posted a sign to say where we were. I'll reopen at four."

"Gee, thanks." I turned to Linda. "I know you have to drive back so Frank can work Thursday, but do you have time to nap first? It's lots of night driving."

She almost pouted. "I wanted to stay until early Wednesday, but I can't blame Frank for wanting to be sure we get home for him to get a good sleep Wednesday night."

Her gaze went to Terry, who was inspecting deserts with Julia. "That little stinker. He likes sweets too much." With eyes only for Terry, she moved away.

Megan raised her eyebrows in my direction. "Wow."

I nodded. "I see you get it." I revised my somewhat critical tone. "She and Frank really helped Terry."

"I'm sure they did. But in some ways, it's good they'll be far away. It might be hard to set the rules if additional people are giving advice."

I grinned. "Other than Aunt Madge, of course. Terry told Frank she's his favorite."

Megan laughed as she picked up a nearly empty casserole dish. "She's everyone's favorite."

I watched Linda playfully remove a brownie from Terry's hand and wrap it in a napkin for him to eat later. I hoped I didn't have to worry about playing favorites.

CHAPTER TWENTY-SIX

SCOOBIE AND I INVITED Frank and Linda to our house for a few minutes to decompress after the funeral and lunch. Linda helped me organize the fridge to make room for leftovers, and Frank helped Scoobie and Terry rearrange his bedroom to accommodate the five bankers boxes they had brought up from Florida, plus the one that had been in Terence's trunk.

I heard Scoobie say, "We'll get those unpacked in a few days. Don't want you thinking you live in a storage unit."

"If I were a little kid I'd make a fort," Terry replied.

I glanced at Linda as she wiped her hands on a towel. "Did he like to make forts?"

She nodded. "Mostly blankets over card tables." Her eyes brimmed.

"He can visit, you know."

215

She turned her back to me. "It's not the same."

I spoke softly. "I know. I can't say I'm sorry. I'm glad he found us. But his life will be...enriched by continuing to know you."

She blew her nose on the dish towel and turned, trying to smile. "Won't be a good towel to wipe dishes with."

I held out my hand. "I'll stick it in the hamper."

Frank's voice carried to the kitchen, "What if we put them behind the futon?"

I didn't hear Scoobie's response because something had occurred to me. I turned to Linda. "What about their furniture?"

She sat at the small kitchen table. "They got rid of some when Marti was sick, to make room for the hospital bed and all that." She glanced toward the kitchen door to be sure Terry could not hear her. "Apparently Terence talked to Terry about starting over here. He'd sold a few things, and the note he left with the boxes said we could call Salvation Army for the rest. He'd even cleaned out the drawers."

"Did you anticipate that level of, what would you call it, cleansing?"

She shook her head. "Frank said you and he talked."

"He mentioned you expected them to be in Florida at least a little longer." I couldn't think of more to say.

Terry called to us from his bedroom. "You guys, come see how it looks."

Linda wiped away another tear and straightened her shoulders as she stood.

"I'll follow you in a minute." I tilted my head. "Potty time."

As I washed my hands, I tried to imagine Linda's pain. I couldn't. I didn't want to set up some kind of visitation schedule. In fact, it would be largely up to Terry. Scoobie and I wouldn't abdicate decision making, but he'd have to want to go.

I dried my hands. It would probably be like kids of divorced parents who lived in different states. The older they got, the less time they wanted to spend away from what they considered their primary residence. That's where they had the most friends and belonged to sports teams.

As I left the bathroom, I heard Linda say, "I thought Terry could show us the diner he and Terence went to that first night. Then we could get on the road."

Frank's tone held forced good humor. "It's a long drive, sweetie. I don't think having a milkshake would help me stay awake."

"So, just Terry and me." She glanced at me as I entered the bedroom, and hesitated before saying, "Jolie could go."

I sensed she wanted alone time with Terry. I couldn't begrudge her that. "I'm really pooped. How about…?"

"Just Terry and me. We won't be long." Linda was almost pleading.

I looked at Terry, who seemed bewildered. "Would you like a quick trip to the diner?"

He looked from Linda to me, and seemed to realize how much she wanted to do this. "I could get a small shake."

"Do you remember how to get there?" Scoobie asked.

"I can drive," Frank offered.

Linda shook her head. "Just Terry and me." She didn't say "one more time" but the implication was clear.

I nodded toward Frank. "I'll make you a thermos of coffee for the car ride."

Scoobie accompanied Linda and Terry to her car, and Frank followed me to the kitchen. "I'm sorry. You guys probably want time to yourselves."

I smiled as I filled the coffee maker's reservoir and added coffee to the filter. "No problem. Besides, I'll sit on the couch while you watch this and fill the thermos." I pulled one from under the sink.

"I hate to take…"

I interrupted him. "Garage sale. For some reason, school lunch thermoses are at almost every one."

By the time Scoobie came in a few moments later, I was lying on the couch.

"You okay?"

I smiled. "It's a good tired. Or a relieved tired. You?"

He tweaked my nose and sat on the far end of the couch. "Much better than I expected. I can't believe how many people came. And the food. What a gift."

I closed my eyes. "I ate half of it."

"Where's your eating-for-two spirit?"

Frank's voice came from the kitchen. "Either of you two want coffee?"

"Don't drink it, thanks," Scoobie said.

"Teeth floating too regularly," I added.

Frank laughed and came into the room with a mug. He sat in the rocker across from us. "I can't thank you enough."

"The other way around," Scoobie said.

I smiled. "I can't believe I got you on the phone that day."

He nodded. "If you hadn't, anyone who answered would have found me right away. Marti and I were good friends."

The next few minutes passed almost painfully. Frank wanted to get on the road, Scoobie and I were ready to be alone. Well, alone with Terry. Our new version of private time.

After Scoobie spent a few minutes describing a couple of our sillier food pantry fundraisers, Frank glanced at his watch. "I better call her."

Scoobie and I exchanged a look, but didn't speak as Frank dialed Linda's cell phone. He frowned and looked at us. "She doesn't answer. Are there dead spots for cell phones around here?"

"Only if you swim out a mile." I swung my feet to the floor. "What about calling the diner?"

"Good idea." Scoobie pulled out his phone. Frank and I listened as Arnie told Scoobie that Linda and Terry had bought milkshakes to go. When he hung up, he said, "The diner staff said the two of them left almost an hour ago."

The three of us were silent for several seconds.

"He might have wanted to show her his middle school," Scoobie said.

"Maybe…" I met Frank's gaze. "Should we be worried?"

He passed his hand over his face and rested it in his lap. "She's been upset, but it never occurred to me she'd drive away with him." He spoke the last words with forced humor.

Scoobie stood. "Tell you what. I know your car. I'll drive around a bit. If they come back when I'm gone, just say I went to the drugstore or something."

"I can..." Frank began.

Scoobie shook his head. "I think if we're both gone it will appear we've gone looking for them. This is probably innocent."

"Besides," I said, "if you're here you guys can get on the road right away."

Scoobie left, and Frank began to pace our small house. At least a few living room laps.

After a couple minutes, I asked, "Can I pack you guys sandwiches for the road? Or some cookies? A bunch were left over..."

"No." He spoke curtly, and then closed his eyes for a second. "Sorry. I guess I'm nervous."

I spoke softly. "I get it."

But I didn't. Until I saw his level of concern, I'd just assumed that Linda had stretched her time with Terry. Now I wondered if she really thought she could simply leave with him. *That's silly. You're being a worry wart.*

I used the excuse of a bathroom visit to be alone.

The front door opened. I finished drying my hands and left the bathroom, expecting Linda and Terry.

But it was Scoobie, and he looked worried as he shrugged off his jacket. "I drove through most of town. Of course, if they were driving too, it would be easy to miss them." He looked at me and I shook my head and shrugged.

Scoobie gestured to the couch. "Have a seat, Frank."

He did. "She's upset. But she wouldn't hurt him."

I said "of course not" and Scoobie nodded.

"But would she try to take him back to Florida?" I asked.

Frank rose again and walked to the front door to open it and stare out the storm door. "I can't believe she'd do that."

I looked at the clock. "It's only been an hour and twenty minutes."

Scoobie spoke sharply. "It's too long." He nodded at Frank. "I don't want to make some official police report but..."

"We could call Dana," I said.

"Who's he?" Frank asked.

I felt hot and took off my pullover sweater. "A she. A sergeant who is also a friend."

"Like for advice?" Frank asked.

Scoobie already had his phone out.

I HADN'T BEEN SURE Dana would come. She could have said to call the station and make a formal missing person report. An Amber Alert, I thought.

But Dana did come. Unlike when in uniform, her brown hair fell loosely to her shoulders. In civilian clothes, she always looked not only approachable, but attractive.

Scoobie introduced her to Frank and took her coat. As he gestured to the couch, he said. "It may be nothing. But it's been an hour and forty minutes."

Dana took a small spiral notebook from her purse. "And what did you expect?"

I shrugged. "Half an hour?"

Frank nodded.

Dana looked at him. "I talked to Madge at the funeral this morning. She explained how much you two did for Terry."

Frank's hands were sweaty and he wiped them on his slacks. "And we'd do it all again."

Dana nodded. "And what is your wife's mental state?"

I wanted to say grief-stricken, backed into a corner, something like that. I didn't.

"She's...terribly sad," Frank said. "Not just about Terry, but because we lost a child to miscarriage a few months ago."

"Ah. And she loves Terry," Dana said.

"With all her heart."

"But nothing about her behavior tells you she would hurt him?" Dana asked.

Frank stared at Dana. "I keep asking myself the same question. The answer is always no."

Dana nodded. "What if Terry wanted to come back. Would she turn the car in this direction?"

Frank's eyes were moist. "Not as clear to me."

My stomach roiled and I went to the kitchen. No one said anything until I came back with a sleeve of saltine crackers.

Dana's smile was tight. "Looks like fun. Listen, you don't have to sit in here, if it's too stressful."

"Not stressful. I...I'm sorry Frank. I'm scared." Once I said it, the whole situation really hit me. Terry was smart, but he had no money, no phone. Unless he jumped out of a car, he'd have no other option. And if he sensed Linda was unhappy, he wouldn't leave her.

Scoobie was saying something to Dana when I interrupted. "First thing tomorrow, we get Terry a mobile phone."

Dana smiled. "Good for even kids his age to have them for emergencies."

Frank rubbed his neck. "What should we do?"

Dana thought for a moment. "We don't think she would hurt him, but she promised to have him back some time ago…"

"Actually," Frank said, "we were supposed to leave for Florida as soon as she returned. We're going to drive some tonight and some tomorrow."

Dana sat up straighter. Her eyes found mine. "The only way we can really help is to get some of the others looking for them. Doesn't have to be an Amber Alert right away. But we need more eyes."

Scoobie nodded. "Frank, do you have a picture of the two of them?"

"Linda has…but the suitcases are in the car."

I snapped my fingers. "I asked the funeral home to scan the photos Terry had on the board. One had him and her. It looked recent."

"Get it," Dana said.

Within fifteen minutes Sergeant Morehouse and two patrolmen were in the house. The funeral home had emailed me all of the photos they'd scanned, and I printed the one of Linda and Terry. Frank wrote the car's color and license number on the copies, and I handed them to Dana to distribute.

Morehouse gave instructions. "For the next half-hour, drive around. Walk the boardwalk. Not too many businesses open, but a few."

Dana added, "He started middle school here yesterday. I wouldn't go in the school yet, but see if the car is there."

Frank looked hopeful. "Yeah, maybe he's showing her his school."

Not likely, I thought, but I gave him what I hoped was an encouraging smile.

The two patrol officers left, and Dana turned to Frank. "What kinds of things did Linda do with Terry? For fun?"

"Mostly he hung with us, she took him to visit friends or play soccer with them after school. He did like Pier Park in Panama City, just to hang out."

"Amusement rides?" I asked.

"More just small shops. I guess there was a train, and a couple small rides. Mostly he and Linda walked around and ate at a couple places there."

"Nothing outside is open now," Dana mused.

"There's more open on the Asbury Park Boardwalk," I said, "but would Linda even know to go there?"

Frank shook his head. "Someplace they could just hang out …"

Morehouse, Scoobie, and I said, "The Mall."

Dana nodded. "They have that food court, and a small arcade if he's into games."

"Jolie," Morehouse said, "why don't you and Frank here…"

I shook my head. "She's jealous of me. I think it should be Frank and Scoobie. I'll stay here in case he calls."

"Terry knows your phone numbers?" Dana asked.

I nodded. "I wrote our home and cell numbers on the back of one of Aunt Madge's Cozy Corner business cards. Terry carries a small canvas wallet."

Frank nodded. "He does." He stood. "You okay with this, Scoobie?"

He stood more slowly. "Jolie, why don't you call Madge and Harry, I guess George and Ramona. George knows every inch of town. He can drive around, too."

Morehouse went back to the station to check accident reports, and Dana stayed with me. I called George and Aunt Madge, but not Ramona. I knew she'd gone back to work after the funeral. Her boss, Roland, would certainly let her leave, but Terry's absence could quickly become known beyond our family and friends.

My cell phone rang. "Aunt Madge," I said to Dana.

"I didn't see the car at the hospital, but I checked the gift shop and cafeteria anyway. I'm going over to Harvest for All."

I relayed Aunt Madge's findings to Dana. "I wish I could do something besides sit."

Dana smiled. "Somebody needs to be here. That's doing something."

AN HOUR LATER OUR small house teemed with helpful people, but no one had spotted Linda and Terry. Nor had Megan seen them. I didn't think Terry knew we hung out at Java Jolt, but I phoned Megan. On a quiet winter day, she would notice people walking on the boardwalk.

Aunt Madge put a tea kettle on, George and Morehouse studied George's big map of Ocean Alley, and poor Frank's coloring had gone ashen. His hands shook as he drank coffee.

I tried to smile with encouragement. "Next cup decaf."

He glanced at his hands and put the mug on a small table near the front door.

Motion near our bedroom door caught my eye. Jazz's head peered around the doorjamb. Unlike Pebbles, she isn't usually shy, but our full house worried her. She wandered from our room into Terry's.

Morehouse raised his voice. "Okay everybody, pull up a chair."

Harry grabbed two from the kitchen and Scoobie brought in the desk chair. I stayed rooted to the couch, and Aunt Madge sat next to me.

When we quieted, Morehouse said, "It's been too long." He nodded at Frank. "I'm not saying Terry is in any real danger, but your wife has to know you all would be worried."

Brakes squealed out front, and a car door slammed. But it wasn't Linda. Lester strode up the front steps and entered without knocking. He eyed all of us. "I seen Megan at the coffee place."

"Come on in, Lester." Scoobie gestured to the one empty chair.

"I been around town the last couple hours, showin' houses. I woulda recognized Terry and the dame from the funeral."

Morehouse frowned. "I know you don't want a lotta hubbub, but we gotta make this official. Let some of the nearby towns know. A localized Amber Alert is the best option. Gets the hospitals checkin', too."

Frank rested his elbows on his knees and put his head in his hands. He raised his head and whispered, "I know she'll be back."

"Probably," Scoobie said, "but we need more people looking." His red cheeks reflected how often he'd gone outside, and his expression was drawn.

I wished I could do something to bring Terry back to him.

George spoke. "Can you tell the other cops to call here if they see her? If Linda and Terry have stopped someplace, I mean."

"If it's close by they can call here. Mostly, at this point, it's gonna be people who don't know any of us. They'll go up to her." He turned to Frank. "No past violence?"

"God, no."

My stomach clenched and bile rose in my throat. Not like morning sickness. It was pure fear. What if Linda decided that if she couldn't have Terry no one could? I tried to push the notion aside, but it kept flitting through my brain.

Aunt Madge turned to Harry. "Do you think one of us should stay at the Cozy Corner?"

He nodded. "I just thought that." He said good byes and left.

Frank said, "She liked it there. And Terry certainly does."

"I'll get the local alert goin'." Morehouse pulled out his cell phone and walked toward the back door to bark orders to someone.

Scoobie had picked up on my rising fear and sat next to me. He slung an arm over my shoulders. "He'll be back soon."

I didn't trust myself to talk.

Aunt Madge nodded to Frank. "What can I do for you, Frank?"

"I wish I knew." He spoke barely above a whisper.

Lester had been quiet, but now he looked around the room. "Where's Ramona?"

I glanced at the clock. "It's four, she should be getting off work. I'll call her."

Morehouse had finished his call and was coming back to us when a car pulled into our small driveway and a door opened and closed quickly.

I beat everyone to the front door. Max had exited the driver's door of Linda's car and was hurrying to the front passenger door. He still wore his reindeer hat, but the antlers had fallen off.

Hot tears of relief ran down my cheeks as a tired-looking Terry got out of the back seat and waved at us.

Frank and Scoobie bounded out of the house, but my strong feeling of relief was almost overpowering – and exhausting.

Behind me, Lester said, "We really gotta get you a bigger house."

CHAPTER TWENTY-SEVEN

SCOOBIE HAD GONE TO THE POLICE station with Frank and Linda late Tuesday afternoon. Aunt Madge stayed with Terry and me. When Scoobie returned, Harry joined us for a supper of leftovers.

After Terry insisted he was fine, we told him he didn't have to talk about his time with Linda. To my consternation, he took us up on that. He sat on the sofa for almost an hour, with Jazz alternately on his lap or pressed next to him.

Probably the stress of the day helped Terry sleep well. Or maybe he didn't sleep. Maybe he stared at the ceiling for ages, too.

Certainly, he was the most alert of the three of us the next morning. He had missed school Tuesday for the funeral, but we thought we should talk before he went to school on Wednesday.

We sat, mostly silent, at the breakfast table. Finally, Scoobie said, "Terry."

He looked up, but then went back to moving pieces of pancake around his plate. He didn't look at Scoobie or me.

Scoobie tried again. "It's sometimes okay to keep feelings to yourself, but your, uh, time with Linda last night was pretty unusual. We want to be sure you're okay."

He sighed, but didn't look up. "She kept saying she loved me. I already knew that."

Scoobie and I exchanged glances, and Scoobie said, "I think she was also really sad about leaving you."

He nodded. "It was kind of like when her baby went to heaven. She was," he looked up, "really nervous or something."

"And probably sad." I touched my stomach. "Babies are so small early in the pregnancy that you can hardly see them. But you still think about your child all the time. It could be hard for other people to understand how she felt about losing her baby."

His fork clattered on the plate. "And that's weird. People keep saying she lost it, and nobody looked for it to, I don't know, put it back in her tummy."

I couldn't believe no one fully explained what a miscarriage was. Or maybe Terence or Frank did, but he hadn't absorbed the enormity of it.

"Uh." Scoobie looked at me.

"It's not lost in the sense of being misplaced. The baby simply doesn't grow long enough to be born. I guess people say 'lost' because they're so sad it could not be born."

He picked up his fork and stabbed a piece of pancake. "She hugged me a lot."

Scoobie and I had discussed what to say, but his focus on her miscarriage had thrown us off course. I refocused. "Linda was also sad that you left."

He rolled his eyes. "I *know* that."

"But," Scoobie said, "her sadness, grief maybe even, are not an excuse for having you away from us for several hours."

In a quieter voice, Terry said, "I know that, too." He looked from Scoobie to me. "I guess it means I won't visit them."

She scared him.

"Certainly not soon," Scoobie said. "But you also need to understand that what Linda is going through now is…a mental health thing."

"Like PTSD?"

Scoobie held his hand palm down and wiggled it back and forth. "Similar. Her grief impaired her judgment. That doesn't mean it always will."

"People can get better," I said.

Terry's expression said he didn't think so.

Scoobie shrugged toward me. "We told you how mean my mother was. I used to have some…problems, too."

"Did you ever kind of kidnap a kid?"

I winced internally. He had not used that term before.

"No. I did skip school in high school, and dropped out of college. I thought nobody cared about me."

We had decided we would not use as an example Scoobie's pot affinity that had landed him in the county jail for a brief time. For selling joints. Later, we could discuss that.

"Huh." Terry looked at me.

"I didn't know him too much back then. Ramona did."

"And Aunt Madge, some," Scoobie said. "But she wasn't Aunt Madge to me then, just Mrs. Richards."

Terry frowned.

Scoobie leaned forward. "I went to those same kind of anonymous meetings your...our Dad did. Right now, Jolie and I just want you to know it's okay to feel confused or angry. And I hope you understand that how Linda acted last night was not her usual behavior."

"I know that. Are you saying you want me to visit her?"

"No," I said. "We're saying please don't judge her forever on how she acted last night. Whether you visit the Bookers, or we have them here again, is a decision for another day."

"It's fine to still love them," Scoobie said.

Terry ate his last piece of pancake, but kept his eyes on the plate. "Who's driving me to school?"

Footfalls came quickly up our front steps. I looked at Scoobie, and he shrugged.

I walked toward the front door as someone knocked. I parted the curtains on the door and smiled as I opened it. "Aunt Madge. Come in."

Terry's chair scraped back and he almost skipped to the foyer, a big grin on his face. "Are you taking me to school?"

Aunt Madge bent to kiss his cheek. "I'd love to. I came to bring you something before school." She handed him a plastic bag that held an item about the size of a paperback.

Terry took it and removed it from the bag. A picture frame. His smile broadened, and he held it up so Scoobie and I could see.

I'd forgotten about the photo of Scoobie, Terry, and me cutting the wedding cake. "Oh, that's terrific!"

He handed it to Scoobie, seemingly for approval.

Scoobie looked at it and grinned at Aunt Madge. "Our next house will need a fireplace with a mantle."

She rubbed her gloved hands together. "Grab your coat and backpack, young man."

Terry ran the few steps to Aunt Madge and hugged her.

Scoobie and I stood in the door and waved as Aunt Madge pulled out of our driveway.

"Did you know she was coming?" he asked.

"No. My guess is she remembered the photo was in her camera and thought it would help Terry. After last night."

Scoobie shut the front door. "I told them I needed to be an hour or so late." He gestured to the living room. "You want more tea or juice?"

I shook my head. "I want our lives to go back to normal."

Scoobie shrugged as he sat next to me. "Whatever that is or will be."

I studied him. "You think we did the right thing?"

"Asking Morehouse not to arrest her?" He nodded. "For now. I think it would have really hit Terry hard if she got arrested."

"Or committed."

"She promised she'd get help."

I shrugged. "If she does, at least she'll feel better."

Scoobie stared at Jazz as she stretched on the carpet in front of the couch. "Morehouse is going to check more records in Florida. He said he can recommend charges later if it turns out she's done anything remotely like this before."

We were silent for several seconds. Scoobie said, "I feel for Frank."

"Me, too. Can you imagine their car ride today?"

"No."

"The pills they gave her at the hospital should help. At least in the short term."

Scoobie shook his head. "Valium. All it does is numb the pain."

"True, but it'll get her home, where she can get more...meaningful help."

Scoobie glanced at the clock above the dining table. "I gotta get going."

BY NINE, I FELT MORE sanguine. The three of us needed time to adjust to the newness of living together. Some days would be harder than others. Surely, there would be less drama as of today.

I smiled, thinking of Max. Who would have thought he could think through the options to find Terry? When he heard from Megan that Terry and Linda had not returned, Megan said he sat still for about five minutes, then left Java Jolt. He found them at the far end of the boardwalk.

One of the few things Terry told us was that he asked Linda if he could show her the boardwalk rides.

Scoobie had shown Terry the closed amusement area on Sunday, and he thought we might look for him there. That told us how scared Terry had been.

When I had asked Max last night what made him search that portion of the boardwalk, he simply said, "I like the rides. I thought Terry would." His biggest concern was that he didn't have a driver's license, and Linda had said she was tired and asked him to drive the three of them back to our house.

After the turmoil of the last few days, the prospect of appraising houses, helping Terry with homework, and trying to burn fewer meals seemed appealingly ordinary.

I stopped by the office to pick up a file for an appraisal in one of Ocean Alley's ritzier neighborhoods. Harry hadn't arrived yet. He's pretty much a nine-to-three man unless we're busy, so I read the file while lying on the couch on the other side of the foyer from our office.

The Hanson home was built in 1938 and had been on the market only twice since then. Because it was the only mission-style home in Ocean Alley, I would not find truly comparable sales to help establish the home's value. I had my work cut out for me.

A local bank requested the appraisal. They know how scrupulous Harry and I are, so I figured they would trust our judgment. I sighed. To come up with the house's value, I would have to compare single-family Victorian homes and maybe one of the huge new cottage-style homes that are set a block back from the shore on the north side of town. I wouldn't put my money into a house almost on the ocean, but people have different risk tolerances.

After I finished reading the file, I borrowed the expensive camera Harry keeps locked in his desk. I'd probably need a wide-angle lens for the interior photos.

A note in the file said the homeowner was expecting me for the nine-thirty appointment. When I pulled in front of the house, I was surprised to see lights on and several people in the living room. Usually owners want the house free of clutter and people. I groaned inwardly. If a lot of people talked to me, the appraisal visit would take longer.

When Susan Hanson let me in, I realized the people were health care workers who must have been attending to someone in the house. It looked as if two of the three were leaving.

Susan didn't introduce them, but guided me directly to the kitchen. "I'm sorry, Jolie, the health team is training a new home care worker for us."

"No problem at all. Can I assume you want to be in your, uh, patient's room when I measure and take photos?"

For a woman of about sixty, Susan had a wrinkle-free, almost placid expression. Now, however, her brow furrowed. "No, but I didn't think about photos in Chester's room."

"I won't take any pictures of him. I'll try to avoid medical stuff. Maybe I'll move a couple of items. I do that sometimes, and then put them back."

Her expression eased, and she told me to take my time. I studied the back of her petite frame and hoped she had help with any heavy lifting.

The Hansons decorated their home in keeping with the clean lines of mission architecture, so it was not hard to measure and photograph the rooms on the first floor.

The second floor had four bedrooms and two baths. I saved Chester's room for last, and knocked quietly on the door.

A woman's voice softly said, "Come on in."

I took in the hospital bed, assorted tables with pill bottles, and antiseptic smell. The latter didn't do my stomach any favors. The fortyish woman who sat in an easy chair next to the bed wore pastel scrubs and a smile.

"Hi, I'm Clarice. Mrs. Hanson explained who you are."

"Will what I'm doing wake Mr. Hanson?"

She shook her head. "Not much does now. If he stirs, he'll go back to sleep quickly."

Clarice was an affable sort. When I explained I needed to take a photo of at least part of the room, she rolled the bedside table full of pill bottles to one side of the room and opened the shades so the room would look cheerier.

I thanked her when I was done. "Sorry if I made your day harder."

"Not at all. I appreciate the diversion." She glanced at Mr. Hanson. "Poor lamb doesn't speak anymore."

It wasn't until I was transferring the photos to our office computer to complete the appraisal report that I had an epiphany of sorts. Linda Booker worked as a home health aide. She probably had access to all kinds of patient medicines. Maybe one of the people in her care didn't get all the digitalis they were prescribed.

I COULDN'T CALL SCOOBIE AT work to explore my theory. I never called him there unless something was almost urgent.

My fifteenth look at the kitchen clock told me it was close to noon. I would pick up Terry at two forty-five and Scoobie would be home about three-fifteen. Time would pass no faster if I paced or watched the clock.

I did a load of laundry and moved a couple extra hangers from our closet to Terry's. With all the furniture moving yesterday, a few dust balls had escaped from under the futon and moved around the hardwood floor as if they owned it.

I grabbed the dust mop from a closet near our back door and sprayed it with some furniture polish so dust would adhere better.

My first swipe under the Terry's futon rousted Jazz, and she was not pleased. "You've never slept under the futon. How would I know you'd be there?"

Tail up, she left the room, probably in search of Pebbles. I called after her. "I get it. You like Terry."

My second swipe hit the two suitcases that belonged to father and son, so I hauled them out while I wielded the duster. I put Terry's back, and paused with my toe on Terence's. Terry had wanted to be sure he had it. Would anything in there tell us more about Terence?

I knelt and jiggled the closure. Unlocked. I swung up the lid and peered in. The jumble of clothes and toiletries reminded me that Morehouse and his crew had gone through the suitcase.

Red plastic in the left corner caught my eye. Moving a shirt revealed a food container, and I smiled. It was the same as Terry's plastic pan of Linda's M&M cookies. *I should probably get rid of whatever's in there.*

Something tickled my brain and I opened the container. Terry had said his dad didn't like the M&Ms so Terence's cookies had none. What they did have was a couple white specks in the middle of a partially eaten cookie. At first I assumed some flour had not been fully mixed into the dough. Then I remembered the pill bottles at the Hanson house.

SERGEANT MOREHOUSE WAS INTRIGUED but skeptical. "You say Linda loved Terry, but she maybe tried to off Scoobie's old man?"

"I feel bad even making the suggestion. But she had expected to become Terry's new mom, and she probably had access to digitalis. Can't you at least check it out?"

I sat in one of the two uncomfortable wood chairs across from Morehouse's desk in his very cramped office in the police station. When he glanced at a stack of files on his desk, I knew he had a lot to do. But we needed to know what was in those cookies.

He accepted the plastic box as I passed it across the desk, and grumbled, "Nothing like a crappy chain of evidence."

"I get that. And even if there is digitalis in these cookies, it doesn't prove she put it there."

"No, it don't. Probably wasn't the tooth fairy either." He peered in. "If she did it, she was pretty stupid. The kid could easily have been in a car with him if he passed out, or whatever."

I shook my head. "Something Frank Booker said made me think they didn't expect Terence to leave when he did."

Morehouse picked up the phone on his desk and dialed. I could hear the person on the other end say, "Ocean Alley Hospital. How may I direct your call?"

Morehouse asked for Dr. O'Malley, and she picked up quickly. "I need you to look at some cookies," he growled.

CHAPTER TWENTY-EIGHT

AFTER HE FINISHED HIS HOMEWORK that evening, Terry explored our relatively small pile of DVDs. "You can buy the Star Wars movies used, like at Goodwill. Did you know that?"

I smiled. "We can think about that."

Scoobie looked up from his copy of Harper Lee's book, *Go Set a Watchman*. "What's your favorite movie?"

Terry flipped through the last couple of DVDs. "How come you don't have any Scooby Doo movies?"

Scoobie shut his book. "What makes you ask that?"

Terry looked puzzled. "Dad said they were your favorite. But you had the old ones. VHS tapes. Dad and me rented copies of the DVDs at the library."

Still absorbed in his stack of DVDs, Terry didn't see Scoobie look at me before he said, "So, I guess I never thought to buy the DVDs."

Terry frowned. "I'm sorry those kids made fun of you. About spelling your name."

I could tell Scoobie had no idea what Terry was talking about, so I asked, "I guess I don't know that story. What do you mean?"

Terry looked to Scoobie, who busied himself with his book. "The kids at school made fun of Scoobie because he wanted to be called a dog's name." He grinned. "So he changed the spelling. Get it? The dog has a 'y' at the end of his name."

I tilted my head in Scoobie's direction. "No one can say that husband of mine isn't smart."

TERRY INSISTED HE WAS wide awake when Scoobie said that nine o'clock on a school night was a good time to read in bed to prepare for sleep. He didn't like the idea, but since he was still figuring out how to protest our guidance, he agreed. Within ten minutes he was out.

Scoobie carefully removed the beat-up copy of *A Child's Garden of Verses* from his grasp and turned on a nightlight. Before we could shut the door to his room Jazz had settled onto the foot of the futon, but next to the wall, so I'd have to lean across Terry to grab her.

I decided to let her have her spot tonight and check with Terry tomorrow to see if he wanted her company on a regular basis.

We stood in the doorway and watched Terry for several moments. Scoobie shook his head slightly. "The kid knows my story better than I do."

I leaned into his shoulder. "Your father must have talked to him about you a lot."

"But he only just told him about me."

"It was a long ride from Florida."

He nodded, slowly. "But they had to have watched Scooby Doo together even before that."

"I'm sure we'll hear more about it later." I studied his profile. "Do you remember naming yourself Scoobie?"

He shook his head. "Kind of. Not really. I think I thought Scooby Doo was brave. Or something."

I kissed his shoulder.

He grinned. "It's possible I'll need some regression hypnotherapy."

"Oh my. Well, whatever you need."

He snorted. "I wouldn't do that. I'll remember more, or I won't."

He paused for a moment before continuing. "It was a traumatic time." He stared at Terry for several seconds. "Can you believe we have a kid? I mean, he's my brother, but he's really our kid."

"Since our eyes don't deceive us, I believe it. Did I imagine we'd be parents this quickly? No." When Scoobie said nothing, I nodded at the group of six white bankers boxes stacked along the far wall. "I want to have this look like a bedroom. Why don't you grab that top one, the one that says paperwork?"

Scoobie raised his eyebrows. "That's the one that was in Terence's trunk."

"So maybe it means it's important."

His expression showed skepticism. "Don't you have enough to do?"

"Plenty. But we also need to get this house ready to sell, so we need a lot less clutter. I can't imagine Terry needs to be with us to go through a box marked 'paperwork.'" I didn't say so, but I thought there could be important information in the box – material on his will, insurance, or bank accounts.

"Anything for my bride." Scoobie took the top box from the stack and carried it to the dinette table in the living room. "This was the only thing in the trunk of Terence's car."

I shut the door to Terry's room and grabbed a paring knife from the kitchen to cut the packing tape on the box. "Wonder why he didn't leave it to be shipped? Want me to start going through this? I can holler at you if something looks important."

Scoobie shook his head. "You're trying to protect me."

"Maybe a little. Why don't you fix us some tea and I'll separate what's in here by subject. Or whatever makes sense."

He shrugged. "Whatever floats your boat." He turned on the burner under our tea kettle while I sifted through the box's contents.

A file labeled 'legal papers' included such things as Terence and Marti's wedding certificate and her death certificate. One marked 'insurance' had life insurance policies for both of them. Hers was marked 'paid' and his was in a sealed envelope. I left that one for Scoobie to look at first.

I was floored by a folder marked 'USAF Pensions.' A quick read made me think that Terry could get child survivor benefits until age eighteen. Perhaps $350 per month. I held up that folder. "I think we'll be able to save plenty for Terry's college."

Scoobie sat two mugs of tea on the table and took the file. "Wow. I can feel some of those gray hairs I thought I was getting turning back to brown."

"And Lester said we should check with Social Security about benefits for him. I forgot about that. Oh!" I flushed. "I also forgot to tell you something else."

Scoobie shrugged. "And I probably forgot three things this week, at least."

"No, I mean, something important." I took a breath. "Sam Jefferson said that when he drew up papers, you know, when your dad wanted to get custody..."

Scoobie shrugged. "If he really wanted me."

"Sam said that your mom got a monthly child support payment. From your dad's disability pension."

Scoobie simply stared at me, and his tone was sarcastic. "She never thought to tell me that."

"I'm sorry, Scoobie, I meant to..."

He shook his head, and smiled. "I told you about those sorry things. Besides, it...helps to hear that. Thanks." He grinned fully and nodded at the box. "It's good. And you do have that box to dig through for more surprises."

I reached back into the box and took out files labeled medical stuff, Terry's school transcripts –wish I'd had those on Monday – and, finally, one named simply Scoobie.

"Uh-oh. Here's one you should open, I guess."

Scoobie took it, turned the folder over, and passed it back to me. "Not sure if I want to do this tonight. You look first."

I opened the folder to see several pages of neatly written text. Obviously a letter. I looked at the opening lines. "Tone is friendly."

Scoobie took back the folder, removed the letter, placed the lid back on the box, and sat the letter atop it. "Might as well read it together."

Dear Scoobie –

I heard you kept that name. I'm glad.

My hope is that you won't read this letter. If you never get it, it means we had a chance to talk.

I'm sorry I couldn't take you with me. I really did try. Nowadays, people know the medicine can help, and I think I would have a better chance. I should have tried harder. Or come back. She said if I tried to see you she would take you away and I'd never find you. Still, when I got better, I should have tried.

When I was in treatment the last time, the time it more or less took, I met Marti. I had no idea people could love each other the way we did. We didn't plan to have Terry, but you've met him. You know he's the best thing that could happen to anybody. He's smart and funny. A lot like you.

I am ashamed to say that I didn't tell Marti about you until right before she died. I guess it was the guilt. Or maybe I was afraid that if I did find you, you would want nothing to do with me, and then Marti wouldn't.

I told her because she kept asking what would happen to Terry if I died. Before I told her, the lady at the library here in Florida helped me look up newspapers and such. I didn't know your mother died, or that you got so bad hurt when that guy beat you up. Please believe me when, like a coward, I say I would have come to help you if I'd known.

We found a picture in the paper, when you got out of college last year. I have no right to tell you this, but I'm so proud. And I saw a photo of you handing out food to people last Christmas.

That's the one I showed Marti. She said you smiled like me. You probably don't want to hear that.

I promised Marti I would bring Terry to meet you. I was going to do it when school was out. Tell him we were taking a vacation to where I grew up.

But then I found out about the cancer. It might be from Agent Orange exposure, or just bad luck. I hadn't had my prostate checked in years. Stupid. At first I thought I'd be okay until after school was out. But the doc said I shouldn't wait. It went to the kidney, because the prostate grew and touched it. Or something. The doctor said you should be checked regular.

I had to tell Terry. I didn't plan to tell him about you until we met, but he cried so hard when I had to tell him the cancer spread. See, the doctor told me I had a few weeks or a couple months. It's funny, but except for the pain sometimes, I didn't feel that bad. I needed to give Terry some hope.

He has been so happy to find out he had a brother. I called the church where the food group you work with is. Thought they might have your phone number. They had your Jolie's number, and the reverend I talked to said he was sorry he was going to miss the wedding New Year's Eve. I fibbed about who I was. Don't blame him for not telling you we were coming. He didn't know.

I'm counting on you now. It isn't fair. All I can tell you is that for everything you may think you do for Terry, he's doing more for you.

Like I said, you shouldn't be reading this. If you are, tell Terry the people he loves are always in his heart.

Love,

Dad (your absent father)

P.S. Another folder has information on insurance. I think it'll be enough for Terry. And you.

I had been so intent in reading the letter that I hadn't looked at Scoobie's face. The tears that rolled down his cheeks were the first I'd ever seen from him. I reached for his hand, but he stood to walk to the window that led to the back porch.

He stood there a few moments, then abruptly turned to enter the kitchen. He tore a sheet from the roll of paper towels and blew his nose.

I stayed rooted to the spot where we'd read the letter. Scoobie already knew I was available for hugs or anything else. Hard as it was, I'd have to wait to comfort him until he was ready.

When he didn't appear in a few seconds, I realized I'd been standing so stiffly my back hurt. I went to the couch and leaned into it. After a minute, I retrieved my now lukewarm cup of tea, then propped a pillow on the couch so that I could lean against the armrest.

How would Scoobie react to what he'd learned in the letter? Understanding his father's many problems might help, but how would he feel about his father not contacting him after he was on a path of recovery? Scoobie knew how hard that kind of road was, and understood the need to ask forgiveness of people you had harmed. Maybe Terence was coming to the Jersey shore in part to do that.

Scoobie had confronted his past directly and made a lot of changes. Of course, he didn't have the burden of knowing he had hurt someone as badly as his father had hurt Scoobie.

I didn't realize I had shut my eyes until Scoobie softly said, "Jolie?"

"Oh. I wasn't sleeping."

He smiled slightly from where he sat on the opposite end of the couch. "Yeah, usually when you sleep your mouth is open a little."

I had a mental image of me with a half-open mouth, grunting as I breathed. "Charming." I studied him for a couple of seconds. "I was trying to give you space."

"Good call." He squeezed the toes of my left shoe. "It'll be a while before I know how to handle all this. Or how much to tell Terry."

"I don't think you have to make any decisions quickly."

He shook his head. "At least I know something different than all the bad crap my mother told me. But I'll never understand…"

"Why he didn't get in touch earlier."

He nodded. "Sam Jefferson talked about my father's PTSD from the war, and I remember how my mother would rage at him. That probably didn't help him any."

I wanted to ask what she raged about, but I supposed it didn't matter.

"I'll just," he began, but stopped as his cell phone rang. "Who would call at nine-thirty at night?"

I shrugged.

Morehouse didn't bother saying hello. "Scoobie. Got something for you."

My face must have shown dismay at what Scoobie used to call my lack of full disclosure. Only this time it wasn't deliberate.

He raised one eyebrow. "Can you give me about five seconds to consult with my wife?"

"Crud. Go ahead."

Scoobie put the phone to his shoulder so Morehouse couldn't hear our conversation. His expression was half-amused, half-angry. "And?"

"I was cleaning today, and when I mopped under Terry's bed, Terence's suitcase was there."

"Been there a few days."

"Here's the thing. I can't explain why I opened it. But I found a plastic tub of Linda Booker's cookies. Without the M&Ms, the way Terry said his dad liked them."

"I repeat. And...?"

"I saw white specks. I took it to Morehouse."

Scoobie stared at me, his lips parting as if to say something. Instead he swallowed and spoke into the phone.

"Okay, Sergeant. I'm up to date."

Scoobie turned the phone so I could hear, and pushed speaker. Morehouse said, "Those flecks she saw were tiny bits of digitalis."

"My God," I whispered.

Scoobie shut his eyes and tilted his head back for a moment. He righted his head and opened his eyes. "Now what?"

"I wish I knew. See, Dr. O'Malley, she's the one who looked at it for us. She's ninety percent sure, and she'll send it to a lab. But even if a lab positively identifies it, it don't necessarily mean much."

I frowned in Scoobie's direction. "Why not?"

"Two reasons," Morehouse said. "First, it's a small amount. Maybe he chewed a pill and took a bite of a cookie. Accordin' to the doc."

I started to say something, but Scoobie raised a finger. "Second?"

"Like I told Jolie this afternoon, there's chain of evidence issues. It's not like Linda handed me, or even Jolie, the container. Terry will probably tell us Linda gave him and his dad cookies in different boxes, and Terence kept his in the suitcase. Lots of people could have touched 'em."

Scoobie nodded, almost to himself. "There's a third issue."

"What's that?" Morehouse asked.

"How much do we want to even have this conversation with people Terry loves if you can't prove anything? What will it do to him? To the Bookers' reputations?"

"You're talking like the county prosecuting attorney. They don't want an arrest unless there's a decent chance they can win a case." He sighed. "Nobody's makin' any decisions tonight."

I spoke to Morehouse for the first time. "The Bookers stayed with Aunt Madge last night and left super early this morning. They were going to call us this evening when they got home."

"I forgot they said they'd do that," Scoobie said.

Morehouse spoke sharply. "I don't want you talking to 'em about this."

"No worries," Scoobie said.

"I mostly called in case they were still with you guys. Thought you should know. If they're gone, it don't matter."

"Sergeant," Scoobie said.

"Yes?"

"I thank you for calling us so late, but like we said to Terry a few minutes ago, bedtime."

Morehouse snorted. "Tell your wife she better start cluein' you in." He hung up.

My face flushed. "Scoobie, honest, I wasn't keeping...'

He waved a hand and then leaned into the couch so he faced the room rather than me. "There's too much going on, and Terry was around 'til a bit ago." He turned to give me a wan smile. "And you're preggers and tired."

I scooted down the couch to sit next to him, and rested my head on his shoulder. "Thanks for understanding." I blew out a breath. "What the heck is next?"

"I just want to focus on us and Terry."

I smiled. "Can Lester give us a list of houses to look at?"

Scoobie looked around the living room. "This is the first place that really felt like home to me."

I felt tears coming and blinked.

"But," he continued, "it's too small for three, let alone four."

I watched his humor return.

"I'm thinking a Jacuzzi suite. Maybe a grape arbor in the back. A separate room for Jazz so she can entertain Mr. Rogers and Miss Piggy..."

I leaned toward him and pretended to punch him in the upper arm as the house phone rang. Scoobie shrugged.

"Probably the Bookers. I'll get it."

"Remember what Morehouse told us," Scoobie said.

I didn't need Scoobie's reminder. I'd thought of another way to broach the topic of cookies.

Linda sounded as if she had a head cold. I wondered if she was crying because Terry was here and she was in Florida, or if Frank was still furious with her.

"We said we'd let you know we got home," she said.

"Hope the drive was okay." *How trite can I be?*

"Rain near Atlanta, but otherwise it was smooth. Frank said to tell Scoobie he heeded his advice and we took our time."

I hadn't heard the advice, but it sounded like Scoobie. "Good. Listen, I never did get that recipe. When I was tossing the last couple cookies Terence had in his suitcase, I noted the tiny white specks. Is that crème of tartar?"

Scoobie sat up straight and raised his hands, palms up, in frustration.

Silence from Linda. After several seconds she cleared her throat. "I will definitely send you that recipe. Listen, I'm exhausted."

"No problem. Sleep well."

I hung up and Scoobie stared at me, half angry, half amused.

I shrugged. "I wanted to be sure she didn't sleep well."

He went to the table to retrieve his now cold cup of tea and sat on the couch again. "I'm not sure if I'm super angry or want to laugh."

I shook my head. "They'll never even question her."

"Morehouse and them could figure they'd have a chance to get a confession."

"Terry's disillusioned enough with a woman he thinks loves him like a mother." I lowered my voice. "She said she'd get counseling. Do we really want her in jail?"

"Me personally? No. I believe people can change. I'll ask Morehouse what they found when they looked for any Florida records on her. If there isn't anything else, I just want this to go away."

"And he always tells me how busy he is with other stuff."

Scoobie snorted. "That's because you usually bug him when he wants you to go away."

"I help him."

Scoobie's eyebrows went up. "On a more serious note, what are you going to tell Terry when he sees that container isn't in the suitcase? He looked in there when Morehouse brought it back the other night."

"I thought about that. I'm going to say when I was chasing dust I pulled it out, and smelled something bad. I opened it and found the cookies had mold on them."

"You might get away with that."

"You have a better idea?"

"Yep." He pulled me to him so I sat on his lap, and we kissed for a long time."

"Much better," I whispered.

He touched my forehead with his. "I know you don't want to be thanked, but thank you for being glad to have my little brother."

"There's all kinds of families, Scoobie. Ours is growing differently than we planned, but we'll end up OK."

THE END

TERRY'S M&M COOKIES

½ cup (one stick) softened butter
¼ cup brown sugar (dark for darker cookies)
¼ cup white sugar
1 egg
1 tsp vanilla
1 7/8 cups flour
½ tsp baking soda
½ tsp baking powder
½ to 1 cup of M&Ms, to taste

Blend butter and sugar with large spoon or mixer, then add egg and vanilla and blend.

Add dry ingredients and blend.

Stir in M&Ms with a spoon, so they don't break up.

Optional: add ½ tsp cinnamon or (for Scoobie) substitute butterscotch chips for M&Ms.

Bake at 350 degrees for 12-13 minutes on a light-colored pan. Adjust to 10 to 11 minutes on a dark-colored pan. Cookies should spring to the touch. If a finger leaves a deep indent, cook another minute or two.

WHAT'S NEXT FOR JOLIE?

Jolie Gentil has sworn off butting into other people's business. I know, right? Sounds as far-fetched as finding used bubble gum on Mars.

Her life revolves around her husband Scoobie, her children, and helping run the Cozy Corner B&B. Aunt Madge has decided to enlighten the Jersey shore by running for mayor of Ocean Alley. With her husband Harry as campaign manager, she has little time for baking muffins and serving tea.

Nothing could drag Jolie into hunting a murderer. Nothing. Really.

Except maybe a request from the most unlikely source. Sergeant Morehouse is convinced his nephew is not a runaway. Something had terrified the teenager, but before Morehouse could find out, Kevin is gone.

Jolie has a soft spot for Kevin, who helped Scoobie's young brother Terry adjust to life in Ocean Alley. Plus, she has a feeling that Kevin saw something he wasn't supposed to see at the hospital, when he had his appendix removed.

It's a hunch, and Jolie believes in her hunches. Scoobie doesn't, and Aunt Madge believes Jolie needs a remedial course in minding her own business.

But Kevin's life may depend on Jolie's certainty and her efforts to find him before a killer does.

Underground in Ocean Alley
Early winter 2018

Other Books
by Elaine L. Orr

The Jolie Gentil cozy mystery series.
Appraisal for Murder
Rekindling Motives
When the Carny Comes to Town
Any Port in a Storm
Trouble on the Doorstep
Behind the Walls
Vague Images
Ground to a Halt
Holidays in Ocean Alley
The Unexpected Resolution
Jolie and Scoobie High School Misadventures (prequel)
River's Edge Mystery Series
From Newsprint to Footprints
Demise of a Devious Neighbor
Logland Mystery Series
Tip a Hat to Murder

Books About Writing
Words to Write by: Getting Your Thoughts on Paper
Writing in Retirement: Putting New Year's Resolutions to Work

Many books in large print and audio.
http://www.elaineorr.com
For articles on reading, writing, and publishing, check out Irish Roots Author.
http://www.elaineorr.blogspot.com

Bio for Elaine L. Orr

Elaine L. Orr is the Amazon bestselling author of the Jolie Gentil cozy mystery series, whose ten books are set at the Jersey shore. *Behind the Walls* was a finalist for the 2014 Chanticleer Mystery and Mayhem Awards. The first book in Elaine's River's Edge cozy mystery series, *From Newsprint to Footprints*, debuted in late fall 2015, and was followed by *Demise of a Devious Neighbor*. Elaine also writes plays and novellas, including the one-act, *Common Ground*, published in 2015. Her novella, *Biding Time*, was one of five finalists in the National Press Club's first fiction contest, in 1993. Elaine conducts presentations on electronic publishing and other writing-related topics. Nonfiction includes *Words to Write By: Getting Your Thoughts on Paper* and *Writing in Retirement: Putting New Year's Resolutions to Work*. She blogs on writing and publishing, and teaches online classes on those topics on the Teachable platform. A member of Sisters in Crime and the Indiana Writer's Center, Elaine grew up in Maryland and moved to the Midwest in 1994.

77638372R00148

Made in the USA
Middletown, DE
23 June 2018